NAKED PUEBLO

NAKED PUEBLO

MARK POIRIER

BLOOMSBURY

First published in Great Britain 1999
This paperback edition published 2000

Copyright © 1999 by Mark Poirier

The moral right of the author has been asserted

Bloomsbury Publishing Plc, 38 Soho Square, London W1V 5DF

ISBN 0 7475 4615 0

10 9 8 7 6 5 4 3 2 1

Printed in Great Britain by Clays Ltd, St Ives Plc

FOR ELAINE LANDER AND JOE WETHERHOLD

contents

NAKED PUEBLO

smonoofnk oeftyh aedy

CHIGGER HAS BEEN LYING about the raised lollipop-shaped scar on his neck since the day after he got it, back when he was twelve or thirteen. What really happened was he ran into a barbed-wire fence because the Petronis' dog chased his perverted ass out of their yard the night we were trying to see Mindy undress before she got into her big pink girlie-frilled bed. All Mindy ended up doing was brushing her hair and talking on the phone, and then their dog—his name was Lover Boy—came churning from around front and chased us out of there. Chigger got clotheslined on the barbed wire that separated their land from his mom's, and it cut into his neck. Lover Boy caught up and humped him.

The wound was deep. You could see the slimy white of his windpipe like a fish belly—shining, in a bloody hole. Chigger's mother was too drunk to wake up, let alone take him to the emergency room, so we doctored up the hole ourselves. We found disinfectant-laced petroleum jelly in the medicine cabinet next to a box of crispy old condoms that had belonged to Chigger's dead daddy back when his daddy was alive. I packed some of the ointment into the bleeding neck hole, made the blood stop. Chigger didn't cry. Probably because I wouldn't let him see the hole. I put a Band-Aid over the jelly, and he forgot about it until the next morning, when his hungover mother pointed it out.

"You did it to me with the nail-pulling end of the hammer last night," Chigger told her, "right after I called you a man-at-the-dog-track-screwing whore."

"You deserved it," she said. "I'm your mother. Always remember, I'm your mother."

"Monkey Lady."

"You better zip it, or I'll make another hole in your neck," she said.

"Just try it," he said. "I hid the hammer."

I could only stare into my Raisin Bran. I always ate Raisin Bran, no milk, when I slept over at Chigger's house. They never had any milk that wasn't almost cheese.

"I'll use this." She held up a turkey thermometer and slammed it back on the counter. Then she looked down and started smoothing her fake-tan pantyhose, pointing one toe like a ballerina and pulling her skirt up a little, like she was sexy. She wasn't, and that was back when she had both of her legs. She was Planet of the Apes Monkey Lady with creases that ran from her lips up toward her nose and down to her chin, like her mouth had once been stitched closed with wire.

"You'd take my temperature?" Chig said. "Stupid."

"I'll stick you good," she said.

"Stupid."

The whole argument was stupid. Chigger was six feet two, 225, even back then in eighth grade. Monkey Lady couldn't have done shit to him even if she had tried. He went through puberty before anyone else and reached physical adulthood at age thirteen. In gym class, if Chigger was on skins when we played shirts and skins basketball, no one would go near him because of his size and because of the thick growth of red fur he had all over his body—even on his back. His team always won. I was always on his team.

JUST LAST WEEK, we were out at Hotel Congress, sitting in the Tap Room, getting drunk on fifty-cent Coors and celebrating my good grades. A girl sat down with us, squeezing up against Chigger in our booth.

"All this and hairy, too," Chigger told her over the crackled Johnny Cash from the jukebox.

She had said her name was Montaigne, but I'm sure her real name was something more like Susan or Anne or Rebecca or Linda or Jennifer or Sara. Her eyes were beautifully dark—like little bowls of chocolate pudding. "Hirsute," she said. "Sexy." She scratched her bony elbow. "I must admit I like your hair color." She pushed his bangs off his forehead. His hair was Bozo-red, like his fur.

Montaigne had a 3-D mole above her lip on the left. It looked fake, like she'd made it from rolling up a glob of rubber cement into a ball and sticking it on there and maybe touching it up with mascara or something to make it darker.

I imagined myself kissing her face. The mole would come off in my mouth, and I'd spit it on the pillow and say, What the hell is that? But I shouldn't have thought that because I had gotten married just a few days before. I shouldn't have pictured myself porking Montaigne, not while I was still married.

"How'd you get the scar?" Montaigne asked Chigger, touching her own neck.

"Knife fight," he said blankly.

"Oh, please." She tapped her cigarettes on the table and bit one out, aiming it at Chigger, then me, but neither of us had a light. She looked around the Tap Room like there had to be cooler people to sit with. There weren't. Only grumpy artists and stinky drunks. One guy who smelled like a urinal puck wobbled over from the bar to our little booth. He held a shaky lighter under her smoke, and Montaigne said, "At least someone's good for something around here," only it was hard to understand her because she had a cigarette in her mouth.

"How'd you get the mole?" I asked her.

"I was born with it, dumbshit," she said.

I reached across the table and pinched her mole and tugged. Her cigarette burned my wrist, but I kept pulling. It felt real all right: rooted, part of her face. Her upper lip stretched out like a tent and she screamed, and her cigarette went down my sleeve and burned me more before I let go.

They made me and Chigger leave. The cranky bartender told us that we weren't allowed to ever go back. Montaigne cuddled up to the bartender and laughed at us. We jumped in Chigger's pickup truck and got a case of Miller for really cheap at Liquor Barn on Speedway and drove up to San Carlos Lake.

FIRST YOU SEE the lights of the prison, then nothing, then Globe, then nothing, then San Carlos Lake. Globe was where they used to make asbestos for school ceiling tiles.

People in Globe have gray, loose skin because of it. Some of the real victims have skin that looks like it might slough off at any moment into a pile at their feet. I've seen them before. One out of every five people in Globe is like that. Asbestos babies are born gray, some with flippers instead of hands and feet. I've never seen one of them, only heard about them. That night all we saw in Globe was the Kentucky Fried Chicken and the huge Basha's supermarket. You could buy buffalo meat at the Basha's there. We did once. Basha's was where I first saw asbestos people. They were pushing carts down the aisles, choosing groceries and pretending like they were healthy and normal. The buffalo tasted wrong when we grilled it up at the lake. Too sweet.

The windows of the truck were down, and the empties were jingling around on the floor with all the other trash. The blaring wind through the cab was cool for May, and wettish, and I didn't even care that I was breathing in the poison asbestos fumes from Globe.

Chigger's the best drunk driver I know. Drives better drunk than sober. Only once did he have a problem. He left his shoes and socks at a party in high school and returned an hour later saying he had run over a guy in a satin Wildcats jacket on Pima Street in front of the Y-Our Church of THE WORD. Me and Grace, this girl we hung out with in high school, drove back there with him, and there was no dead guy in a satin Wildcats jacket, no blood on the street, no dent on his truck. "You're really fucked up," Grace told him. "You better just get your ass on home." We helped him into his truck.

WE ROLLED UP to San Carlos Lake at around eleven or midnight. I was drunk when I fell out of the truck and landed hard on the solid dirt. The geezers' sparkling bass boats reflected everything in the sky, and looking at them from down in the dirt, watching them tilt and then correct themselves, watching the sparkles streak in my drunk eyes, I got sick. I staggered over to a blue Port-o-let next to Winnebagos and other bass boats and began chucking up all the Millers into the plastic toilet.

Chigger started rocking the Port-o-let from the outside. All the shit and piss and that blue chemical liquid splashed up at my face and made me sicker and puke more and burned my eyes, but all I could do was grip the toilet. The old bass fishermen's turds and toilet paper and slop came up over the toilet seat and on me, but it was hard to let go while Chigger was rocking the whole thing. I could hear him laughing, and I tried to yell at him to stop, but I couldn't talk. When I reached one hand back to open the door and get out, I couldn't get the latch. I had put the little metal bar through and locked it, and I couldn't stand up to get the leverage to undo it. I just smeared around on the wet, sticky floor while more shit splashed up over the toilet and my clothes got more drenched. All the while I could hear Chigger's laugh. Then he tipped the whole thing. It thudded down, and I landed with my back in the little urinal. I reached over my head and pushed the lock open, and then the door, and stood up, one foot in the urinal, the other foot with no shoe.

I wiped my eyes on my wet shirt. It didn't really help, but I saw Chigger standing there in front of the glittery bass boats, looking like he knew he'd really fucked up, but like he'd never admit it and apologize. He didn't; he just said, "Freddy, you better jump in the water and clean your ass up."

I did jump in. It was warm and kind of thick, but I liked the calm. I could see Chigger. He walked to the edge of the lake, all big like he was. If anyone else had done it to me,

Chigger would have kicked their ass. He's true as hell that way. Loyal. Once he even beat the hell out of my daddy for me—and I didn't even have to ask.

San Carlos Lake is man-made, but bigger than most of the man-made ones. They stock it with bass, and the snowbirds come up and try to fish them all out. Cows walk around the lake. They do laps in herds, like old people in the mall. The shore is spotted with their paddies. Some say that's what the bass eat, but bass eat meaty things like bugs and ducks. Most of the small bass you catch up there act like they've been caught a hundred times. They barely wiggle when you reel them in. They flop once or twice for show, and then they casually open their mouths for you to take the hooks out. I've heard of giant bass that have survived ten or eleven seasons without being reeled in. Once there was a guy up there using kittens as bait, saying he almost caught a fifty-pounder.

It's a big enough lake for the sparkly bass boats, big enough to windsurf if there's wind, but not big enough that it doesn't smell and look stagnant by August. The water is golden at the end of the summer, and at night it's brown like Pepsi. That night, after Chigger tipped the Port-o-let, the water wasn't that bad.

My one bare foot felt the bottom of the lake—loose mud, plants, probably soggy cow paddies—silky and squishy between my toes. "Get over here!" Chigger yelled, but I backstroked farther out and looked at the thin orange wafer of a moon, and I thought about Montaigne and her mole. It had looked so fake. I still think it might be. I kept floating, hearing Chigger yelling, demanding I come back, but not once apologizing for the Port-o-let tip-over. Someone yelled at him to shut up, then I heard a big thud like someone in logger boots had kicked a metal trash can. I wondered what Chigger had done, but I kept swimming and tried to ignore the ruckus. I dog-paddled out to the middle and dove down into the blackness, went deeper, until I felt the pressure in my ears, until I heard nothing but the soothing thrum of my blood pumping through my body. With my eyes open, I saw nothing; not even the moon's rays could work their way down there.

Then I floated for a long time—maybe an hour—and when I finally swam to shore, Chigger was snoring in the pickup. He had found my shoe and washed it off and left it in the bed of his truck with a big oily tarp for me to use as a blanket. I peeled off my wet clothes and hung them all over the truck and wrapped myself up in the dirty tarp and slept in the back of the truck. Gravel and trash poked my back and face all night.

THE GEEZERS GET up early at San Carlos Lake. Near five that next morning, they were all milling around, putting their boats in the water, revving their motors. Chigger was up early, too. I could hear him lying to a man about how he got the scar on his neck from a giant catfish he caught in Louisiana. He said the catfish knocked him off his boat and one of its fins cut him in the neck. "I can still see that fish's evil black eyes," he said, "like death looking right at me."

Chigger lumbered back to the truck, kicking up the dirt with his boots. I pretended to be dead asleep when he got close. I closed my eyes and opened my mouth, worked some drool out with my tongue.

"There's a whore trailer set up on the other side of the lake," he told me.

I opened my eyes. There was no use prolonging it. He was wringing his giant hands, making that sandpaper noise. He shouldn't have been wringing his hands, shouldn't have been excited about the whore trailer. Once, two days after a visit to a whorehouse in Nogales—Casa de Teresita—the chirpers showed up. He was the first person I knew who got them, and they migrated from his pubic bush to all parts of his body on account of his furriness. His armpits were infested the worst. You could hear the lice chirping away like baby crickets, and you could see the little yellow creatures swarming and hopping all over. His whole body and head had to be shaved; he let me do his back and his tender regions. We started with electric clippers and then straight razors and shaving foam. Red fur covered his mother's kitchen floor. No one swept. You can probably still find some soapy clumps of it under the dishwasher. With no fur or hair, Chigger looked like a big marshmallow with eyebrows, like someone rolled him in flour. The fur grew back fast—and thicker, more plush.

"They've got a whore trailer across the lake," he repeated. "This old fucker named Manny was telling me the girl's beautiful, and it's only twenty bucks."

I got up and started to feel my clothes. They were still damp, drenched really. I reached into the pocket of my heavy jeans. The wet dollar bills were there, so I pulled them out. I handed them over, gazing past Chigger to the brown lake, focusing on the glitters of morning sun, trying hard not to let Chigger see how I was feeling.

"Your pants'll be dry before you know it," he said, getting into the truck. "Just keep that tarp around you, and we'll drive over there." He rolled down the window and said to me, "Come on."

I bunched up my clothes into the corner of the bed so they wouldn't blow away when we drove, jumped out of the back, and got in the cab with him. It smelled too much like

Chigger, like he had secreted a lingering musk during the night. The empties were still all over the floor, along with the three we didn't drink. I cracked one of the full ones. It wasn't too warm, and it was wheaty like Miller usually is. I chugged it because I was starved from puking so much.

"How much money do you have?" I asked him as he started the truck.

"Here, look." He reached into his back pocket, and we almost backed into a station wagon parked off to the side of the dirt road that loops around the lake. Like I said, he drives better when he's drunk, concentrates more. He tossed his tooled-leather wallet at me. CHIGGER is branded into it, and white stitching holds it together. Had it since I met him in fourth grade.

I found thirty-seven dollars. He handed me my four wet dollars from his shirt pocket. I looked through the rest of his wallet—mostly just scraps of paper with phone numbers, and charge receipts. He had three credit cards. His Visa was maxed—I knew because he had offered to pay for our hotel bill down in Puerto Peñasco, and the lady tried to keep it and cut it up to get fifty dollars from Citibank. That's what's good about Chigger. He's not rich, but he'll always pay for things. He also had an Exxon card, brown around the edges, and a Levy's card, even though Levy's turned into Sanger Harris and then into Foley's and then into Robinson-May Company years ago. There was a laminated picture of him and his daddy at the Pima County Fair on a kiddie ride where you sit in cars with steering wheels that don't work. It was taken back when Chigger was around six and wasn't gigantic yet, back when his daddy wasn't dead.

"Give me that," he said to me, snatching the wallet. His arms were redwood logs: practically the same girth from his wrists to his armpits, the same size since junior high.

"You have thirty-seven dollars," I told him.

"Then with your four, we have a dollar to spare."

"I might not be into it," I said. "After all, I'm married."

"I forgot about that," he said. "How's Zena treating you?"

"Lena," I said. "She's treating me the same."

"If you don't want to go, I'll go twice," he said. He gassed the truck, and we fishtailed in the dirt. I checked in the back—my clothes were still there. He turned on the radio, but none of the pretuned Tucson stations came in. He played with the knob and stopped at a station where an Indian was reading a legend: . . . *a strange wild beast roams on the sky. It has a head of bear and the tail of a magic snake. With its mighty thrashing tail, it conjures the heavy, hot wind of the tornado . . .*

I started to ask Chigger how he'd know which trailer was the whore trailer, but he told me to shut up so he could listen to the radio.

We pulled up in front of a guacamole-colored Winnebago, and Chigger just sat there and listened to the rest of the monotone Indian: . . . *Honor the beast. Fear the beast. . . .* When it was over, he clicked off the radio and said, "I haven't been laid since Tuesday."

We got out, and I spread my clothes so they'd get sun. I was still wrapped in the dirty tarp, and the gravel hurt my bare feet. I limped along behind Chigger like an old nun. Chigger was at the Winnebago door, pounding, then rocking the whole vehicle. A girl who looked to be around twelve answered the door. She had mussed-up morning hair and wore only a big yellow T-shirt.

"Too early," she said.

"Come on," Chigger said. "I just now heard about it." He was wringing his hands hard. Wormy blue veins showed through the fur on his arms.

"From who?" she asked, folding her arms across her chest.

"Manny. He has a big bass boat."

"Hold on," she said, and shut the door. She opened it a second later. "Pull your truck right up alongside so there's about four feet between. Like an alley."

Chigger ran to the truck and did as she said. The bed of the truck was then in the shade of the Winnebago, and I was thinking: My clothes will never dry.

The girl came back out with a ratty red sleeping bag. She spread it out in the dirt between the truck and the Winnebago, and then walked up to Chigger and me. "Twenty for a fuck, ten for a BJ," she sighed.

"Where's the whore?" I asked her.

"Me," she said. She smiled at me like she was about to laugh, just then noticing I was wrapped in a grimy tarp.

Chigger glared at me. "Stupid sometimes," he said, and socked me in the stomach. Not hard. He looked around and sat in the dirt and pulled his boots and socks off, then stood and stripped off his T-shirt and unbuttoned his Levi's. The girl looked at him like she might look at an operation on The Learning Channel, like she'd change the channel if she could, but then she'd change it back and fully check it out. She began to pet Chigger's stomach. "Soft," she said, "like an orange cat."

He followed her over to the sleeping bag, wearing only his white boxers. She lay down and hiked her T-shirt up over her knobby breasts. Chigger let his boxers fall and jumped on top of her. She disappeared under him, and I decided it was time to stop watching and to think about something else.

An older guy, skinny with a twisted torso and rotten Indian-corn teeth, came storming out of the Winnebago, slammed the aluminum door back. He was yelling at the girl: "Sneaky bitch!" He looked at me and said, "Give the money to me, I'm in charge here." His hair was blond, but darkened with oil and filth. Before I could tell him Chigger had the money, he sucker-punched me in the nose with his bony little fist. The pain bloomed all over my head, and I couldn't see for a second, so I sat down in the dirt and held the tarp up to my face. My nose was burning and bleeding, and my mouth tasted like old pennies, but I had to look up to make sure the guy wasn't going to sock me again. He had gone over to Chigger, which was a mistake. Chigger, with his big angry erection, got up and saw me all bloody, and he socked the weasel-pimp in the jaw from the side. It cracked like green wood, and when the guy turned around, I could see his jaw hanging slack and his eyes rolled white. Chigger grabbed him from behind, put one arm through the guy's legs, and picked him up and spun him over his head before he tossed him like a sack of feed—about ten feet past the girl. The man landed on his face, and I heard another crack. Chig had thrown my daddy like that, too—broke his arm on one side and his wrist on the other. I didn't even have to ask him to do it.

The girl crab-scuttled back on the sleeping bag, pulled her shirt down, and draped the sleeping bag over her head.

A lady with long, white hair slid open a little window in the Winnebago and pressed her face up against the screen. "Git!" she yelled at Chigger, and then she backed up and fired a big gun that blew the screen off and left a blue puff of smoke hanging above Chigger's head. He grabbed his pants, grabbed me under the arm, and we piled into the truck and skidded away.

Chigger was driving the truck naked, swerving all over the place. Neither of us really cared we were naked until we stopped for gas in Globe. My wet clothes had blown away somewhere back by the lake. Chigger wrestled into his pants and started filling the tank.

The service attendant, who I suspected was in the early stages of asbestos disease because of his gray wrinkling left ear, walked over and gawked at Chigger, who had no shirt or shoes. "You look like my sister's Irish setter," he said.

"You look like a gas station man," Chigger said.

The guy didn't respond, just took a twenty from Chigger and gave him his change. Chigger got me paper towels for my nose, which was still dripping a little at that point. It still hurts some if I sneeze, and the punch was last week.

CHIGGER FINISHED AT the University of Arizona in three years. He got a degree in sociology, which is a pretty easy major, but he did it in only six semesters and landed a job right there when he finished. He still has the job. All he does is tell students what classes they need in order to graduate. He has his own office, and he's the youngest assistant to the associate dean ever. Really. Students come into his office, he punches up their Social Security numbers on the computer, and he advises them. Sometimes he has to listen to them complain about unfair grades or read their requests for grade changes. I'm still a student, and he's been changing my grades every semester since he got the job. He's good that way. He does it without my having to ask. He doesn't make fun of me for being in my sixth year. Each time I get my grade report, I'm pleasantly surprised to see that I'm on the dean's list again, and that my cumulative GPA has moved up a little. Then Chigger takes me out and gets me drunk to celebrate my grades, like I earned them myself or something. That's what we were doing the other night when we met Montaigne the mole girl.

He got me an apartment in Scotia Club two years ago, when we were both juniors. Scotia's an adobe complex with

red tile roofs and a huge Olympic-sized pool and sand vol-
leyball courts and Jacuzzis. Usually there's a waiting list to
get one of the apartments, but Chigger knew the guy, and
he got us each one right away. Mine's right above his old
one. Chigger doesn't live in Scotia anymore.

It was great when he did live there; we had our routines,
and the days passed slowly. One night, a year or two ago, like
most of the nights back then, we sat in the Jacuzzi closest to
my apartment with Lena and Zena, my neighbors. Lena and
Zena are twins with clipped-up, huge, wild blond perms and
StairMastered asses. New Jersey girls. They talk funny, kind
of tough, but that makes them cuter because they're not even
close to being tough. They wear fluorescent everything.
Lena was the one I was married to for a short time recently.
That night, the Jacuzzi-talk topic was Brenda, a girl who
lived in 605, the apartment higher than all of ours.

"If she looks at me like that one more time, I'll kick her
skinny ass," Lena said.

"I'll scratch her fucking eyes out," Zena said. Then she
grabbed Lena's right hand and held it next to hers, and asked
Chigger and me which one of them had better nails.

"Sorry, Zena, but Lena's are longer," Chigger said.

"Yours are a better color, though," I told Zena. They were
bug-juice blue.

Chigger used to pork Lena. I used to pork Zena. Then we
switched. Then they told us, "It's getting too weird," so we
stopped. Chigger porked other girls in Scotia. Lots. Not
Brenda in 605. She was afraid of Chigger. She once told me
she thought he was dangerous, a time bomb, maybe in the
militia.

We all had Pacifico Ballenas that night—big fat thick beers
that you have to buy down in Mexico—and we were all grinning with droopy relaxed eyes, breathing in warm chlorine,

and getting wrinkled as we gazed at the purple night sky. The stars were so bright that night that they reflected in the Jacuzzi when the jets were off. We sat extra still and tried to find the Big Dipper backward in the water. We couldn't.

Mexican polka music blasted from a taco truck in the parking lot just as we gave up looking for constellations. Chigger yelled to the taco guy to bring us some food, but he didn't hear. Then Chigger turned to Lena and said, "Did I ever tell you how I got this scar?"

"Did I ever tell you you're a stud," she said. Then she leaned over and separated the fur that surrounded the scar, and touched it. "It's hard," she said, "and pinker than the rest of your skin."

"I hate Jacuzziing with you, Chigger," Zena said. "I find red hairs all over me for days."

"I'm always with you," Chigger said. Then he grabbed Zena by the shoulders and pushed her underwater. We could feel her kicking and squirming around under there. Chigger held her under and watched two guys who were setting and spiking in the sand courts under the floodlights. Lena and I looked at Chigger, but neither of us said anything. I was hoping that he hadn't forgotten about Zena being under-water, hoping that he'd let her up in time, because she was down there for what seemed like too long. Lena started cry-ing, not loud, just tears and red eyes. Finally, Chigger sighed and yawned, and let Zena up.

Zena was coughing and burping out water, and her sur-prised eyes looked gigantic and loose. With her wet hair and those eyes, she hardly even looked like Lena's twin. Then she started laughing and said, "You almost killed me, Chigger. You knew right when to stop." She flipped her hair off her face and jumped on his lap and started kissing him all over, twirling his fur with her tongue.

We were drunk, but safe and warm, and Zena and I had a chemistry final the next morning. We weren't worried about it. We both went to the lecture almost every time, and then there was Chigger to help us with our grades if something went wrong.

Chigger moved out of Scotia Village and into his old bedroom in Monkey Lady's house after she got robbed and gagged and left for dead. "I need to protect her ass," he said.

Chigger and I had gone over to her house one afternoon to look for his old GI Joes to sell to an antique store, even though neither of us was desperate for money. It was probably the first time we had gone over there in months, and his mother was tied up on the kitchen floor, squirming on the dirty linoleum. She had pissed and shit herself a few times, and stank, and from the looks of her face—purple, red, and puffy—the robbers had beaten the dust out of her pretty good. When Chigger undid the ropes and gag, she opened her eyes and said, "Chigger, I'm so sorry about the hammer and your neck," and then she started to bawl.

Chigger helped her up and carried her into the bathroom. The robbers had thrown her fake leg into the green pool, but Chigger didn't find it until after he had bought her another. She had lost her real leg years earlier. It was torn off on the Tilt-a-Whirl at a junky carnival set up in the parking lot of Puchi's in South Tucson. She was drunk, out with her drunken girlfriend Freedah, and decided while the ride was going that she had to have some cotton candy. Her leg got twisted off. Chig told me not to tell anyone how she really lost her leg. He told me to say she had cancer. He didn't like it when people talked about her. He still doesn't. Once, in high school, at lunch, I made the mistake of calling her Monkey Lady in front of him. I had heard Chigger call her Monkey Lady millions of times, but when he heard me say it, he put both his hands around my neck like he was going to strangle me to death. Then he just said, "Not good." No one else in the cafeteria understood. I did. I never slipped up again.

Chigger moved home to Monkey Lady. He was convinced the robbers were coming back. That was a year ago. He still goes out, but he spends a lot of his spare time playing cards with Monkey Lady, making dinner for her, cleaning the house.

SO LENA AND I got married. We had to because they're twins and Zena got married—not to Chigger, though; to Frito, a fat guy who started hanging out with us after Chigger left the complex. Lena and I got divorced earlier this week, when I got back from San Carlos Lake. Zena learned Frito had been cheating on her with three different Scotia girls. Lena and I didn't really want to get divorced, but we hadn't really wanted to get married, either.

We drove down to Nogales for the divorces. Frito didn't come, so we picked up Chigger at his mother's house on the way, and he pretended to be Frito. After we paid the smiling Mexican lawyer twelve bucks for each divorce, we got loaded at Elvira's Cantina on ten-cent shots of tequila from tiny paper cups. Chigger and I left the girls for an hour and went back over to Casa de Teresita.

Yesterday when Lena, Zena, and I went over to Monkey Lady's house for a barbecue, Chigger led me into the pool shed and pulled down his swim trunks. "Hear any chirps?" he said. He pushed my head down there so his ugly dick was right in my face.

"No," I said. "I didn't get them, either."

"We have to go back this weekend," he said, letting my head up.

"You're pushing your luck."

"I like Teresita's," he said. "It's cheap."

"It is," I said.

"And they need our business."

"Yup."

"And you're not married anymore."

"Nope," I said.

Monkey Lady stayed in the house and got drunk during most of the barbecue. She did hobble out once. She sat on Chigger's lap. It was hot that day, around one hundred, and the humid monsoon winds were picking up. Sweat rolled from her stump onto her fake leg and then onto the real sneaker and sock she had on the fake leg. "All the girls gather round. I want to talk about my Chigger," she said. Lena and Zena were the only girls there. "I want you to tell me that my Chigger is handsome."

"He is," Lena and Zena said together, nodding, holding paper plates bending with hamburgers and potato chips. "Hot," Zena added.

Chigger just grinned, turned redder.

"I did this to him," Monkey Lady said, stroking his neck scar with her finger. "I did it with a hammer when my Chigger was just a boy." She started to cry, and no one knew what to say. "I'm so sorry," Monkey Lady said. Then Chigger carried her inside, put her away.

When he came back out, I asked him why he wouldn't just tell Monkey Lady—only I didn't say Monkey Lady—that she didn't give him the scar.

"I've told her a hundred million times," Chig yelled. "She doesn't believe me."

I walked in the house to take a piss, and I saw Monkey Lady sitting at the kitchen table with a bottle in front of her. She had taken her fake leg off, was letting her stump get air.

Her stump was propped up on another chair, and she was fanning it with a magazine.

"I saw Chigger cut his neck," I told her from the hallway.

"I was drunk, and he yelled mean things at me, and the hammer was right there," she said, crying.

"He cut it on the Petronis' barbed wire," I said. "You weren't even there."

"Liar!" she screamed. She threw the magazine at me. It slapped the wall and landed at my feet. "Chigger paid you to say that!" She picked up her fake leg and hucked that at me next. It would have nailed me in the face, but I ducked.

WE WERE KIDS when Chigger kicked my daddy's ass. Chigger and I had been playing Space Invaders when suddenly light poured into the dark family room and made us squint. Daddy stood in the doorway holding my bashed-up bicycle in front of him. Then he heaved it at me and didn't tell me why until after. It was a real cheap BMX model with fake spring shocks and plastic fenders, but I loved it. Chigger and I had recently greased the chain and put on new knobby tires. They still smelled new that day. The pedal struck me in the ear and scraped me down to my chin. My ship on the screen blew up. Daddy had backed his car over the bike on his way to golf because I was dumb and left it in the driveway. "What're you thinking, Freddy!" Daddy yelled at me. Chigger was smart; he had left his bike in the grass. My bike got all tangled under Daddy's car, did something to his muffler.

Right after Daddy threw my bike, he knew he had made a mistake. I could see it in his bugged eyes when he spotted Chigger in the recliner wringing his giant hands. Chigger jumped up, pulled the bike off of me, and chased Daddy out of his own house. I followed, holding my burning ear.

Chigger caught up with him as he was trying to get back into his car. He socked Daddy in the side of the head. The sound the blow made was soft, like Chigger had punched a couch cushion, but my father fell over on the driveway. Chigger picked him up and tossed him, like the two of them were rival professional wrestlers on TV. Daddy landed on the pavement with no noise except for a creepy, wild squawk. He broke his arm on one side and his wrist on the other. His ugly silver digital watch smashed, too, and its liquid crystal leaked in all directions, dripped on the top of his twisted hand. Daddy's arms were just hanging there like a puppet's as he kneeled by my basketball, which I had also left out. He kept looking at his arms like he didn't believe they were his, then looking over at Chigger and me, then back at his arms, then back at us. He slumped down on the driveway like a big baby. As I watched Daddy, all crumbled and confused on the ground, I thought: Thanks, Chigger.

Chigger and I went back inside and played another round of Space Invaders while my mother drove Daddy to the medical center.

Later, at Chig's house, we tried to fix my bike, but it was no use—the frame was bent.

I DIDN'T TELL Chigger or Lena or Zena about Monkey Lady throwing her leg at me. I didn't want to ruin the barbecue fun we were having. We climbed the fence up to the flat roof and lounged in old lawn chairs as we watched the inky clouds bowling over from the southeast. Lightning cracked through the sky and left glowing prints on our eyes. Lena and Zena sipped electric-blue cocktails from Tiki-head glasses and crossed their shiny, tanned legs. Chigger leaped off the roof a few times, barely clearing the cement deck and cannonballing into the pool. After the third time, he flubbed around the pool like a polar bear in a zoo moat. Lena and Zena begged him to get out because of the lightning. Their uncle Shelby had been struck by lightning; they'd seen and smelled the whole thing. Said that they saw the lightning blow a hole in his skull and leave through his eyes and mouth. When they described how his dick burst like a hot dog in a microwave, Chigger finally got out and joined us back on the roof, dripping.

Montaigne arrived. I watched her strut through the gate, saw her mammoth mole from all the way up there on the roof. She wore cut-off overalls and had braided her hair like a hillbilly girl.

"Up here!" Chigger yelled at her. "Get yourself a beer."

Montaigne hustled up with a Coors, and as soon as she saw me, she said, "You so much as look at my mole, I'll rip your balls off."

"Who is this bitch?" Zena whispered with her fruity breath.

"We met her at the Tap Room," I said. The mole clung to Montaigne's face like a swollen tick. I thought it had migrated since I last saw her.

"Stop looking at me," Montaigne said. "Don't think I won't rip your balls off." She sat on Chigger's wet lap and started to curl his chest fur around her fingers. Then she kissed the fur, sucked it into dollops, and played with his scar, like Lena and Zena used to do.

It started to rain then: distinct drops, tablespoon-sized. The roof steamed, and we felt the vapor on our bare legs.

Zena and Lena glared jealous hatred toward Montaigne as the rain *ploop*ed into their cocktails. Chigger grinned like a pervert. Montaigne posed, stared at me with her beautiful chocolate eyes. And I knew that if she tried to hurt me, Chigger would kill her.

before the barbecue hoedown

SHE WAS CALLED Jackpot because when she was born, sixty-one cents' worth of coins slid out of her mother's cooch along with her. A dime was stuck to her forehead, a penny to her right knee. Her mother, Lisbiana, had been a stripper at the Spare Bar in Agua Prieta, where her specialty was making change. Lonely cowboys from across the border in Douglas would insert rolled dollar bills into her, and she'd spit out a coin or two. None of the other strippers was dexterous enough to take over Lisbiana's change-making act when she left with a silver-eyed rancher, so the Spare Bar transformed into just another border-town strip joint with no special attractions. The silver-eyed rancher, CW—Carry Wilcox—drove a wide-hipped Ford pickup and lived outside of St. David. Jackpot got her eyes and her nationality from CW.

CW was already married when he took Jackpot's mother

home—had two wives, little blond, creamy Mormon girls—but in St. David the justice of the peace was accustomed to that sort of thing, he himself being a follower of Joseph Smith. Lisbiana knew enough to get pregnant before she left CW. She had all the marriage papers in order before she departed, the ones necessary to get citizenship. She moved to Eloy and worked answering the phone and filing in the sooty office of a company that shredded tires. She told Jackpot all the details on Jackpot's fifteenth birthday. The girl wasn't at all surprised, she had known her mother was peculiar.

GIRL NEEDED TO *live and work in my home.* Jackpot thought it was probably a pervert who had placed it, a fat guy with pinkie rings and hairy knuckles, but it was the only new ad in Thursday's *Tucson Citizen,* and she wanted out of flyblown Eloy. She hoped to move down to Tucson and make enough money during the summer to attend the university there in the fall. She called the number in the ad as soon as she saw it, and was glad when a woman answered.

"Name?" the woman on the phone asked.

"Jackpot Wilcox."

"That's a strange name."

"So?"

"Do you have any office experience?"

"Yes," she lied.

"Can you come by at two tomorrow? I've got eight girls coming so far."

"Yes," Jackpot said.

"And where are you driving from?"

"Eloy."

"Oh my," the woman said. "You've got quite a haul."

. . .

AFTER TEN MINUTES of talking, Bobbi hired Jackpot and showed her to her room. "You remind me of me at your age," Bobbi said. "You've got spunk. I like spunk. The last girl I had was a lazy Lulu." She led her upstairs. The room Bobbi gave Jackpot was much nicer than Jackpot's own room back home in Eloy: a queen-sized bed, a rolltop desk, and a private bathroom with a huge whirlpool bathtub of swirled green fiberglass.

A fleshy, self-satisfied pig, the color of Silly Putty, strutted out of the bathroom. It ignored Bobbi and Jackpot and continued down the hall, dainty hooves clicking and skidding on the hardwood floor.

"That's Mary Anne," Bobbi said. "She's clean as all get-out. She takes care of her business outside in the desert." Bobbi smiled in the direction of the beast and sighed. "The tenderest pigs are house pigs like Mary Anne. Last year it was Charlene roaming around here."

"We have goats and chickens in Eloy," Jackpot said.

"Then you and Mary Anne will get along fine. She mostly does what she pleases."

"I'll bet she does," Jackpot said.

"This was my husband's room before he passed," Bobbi said. "He was a cripple, all knotted and lumpy with the arthritis. That's why we got the whirlpool bath. Still smells like him in here." She sniffed after she said it. Jackpot sniffed, too. She detected menthol.

Bobbi had frightened Jackpot at first. Her white hair was swooped up and stiff in the shape of a flame. She wore a sleeveless lavender top, and the sun-freckled skin of her upper arms draped loosely off her bones. Jackpot feared her nails the most: hooks, painted bubblegum pink, with glued-on twinkles. But Bobbi's tranquil voice made her less horrific, and it seemed like an easy enough job: answer the business phone, keep the house clean, and help her organize a big barbecue hoedown. Bobbi was a Realtor, "the ninth most successful one in Tucson last year," she had boasted. "The year before I was only the thirty-first most successful Realtor in Tucson. The hoedown I threw for all my clients last summer changed all that." In exchange for her labor, Jackpot got the room, food, and four dollars an hour—under the table. She also got the hell out of Eloy.

"You'll move in tomorrow, then?" Bobbi asked her as she was leaving.

"How about Monday? I have some loose ends to tie up this weekend."

"Monday's super. See you then, honey."

THEY HAD WARNED Jackpot about hanging out with Shana. The teachers called Shana too sassy for her own britches. One had even said that reputations were contagious. That was in eighth grade, five years ago. Jackpot hadn't contracted a reputation yet, at least not one like Shana's. After she got the job from Bobbi, she stopped in at the Dairy Queen to tell Shana the good news.

"Things always fall your way, Jackpot," Shana said. "Makes me sick." Shana was stooping behind the counter, dipping a large vanilla into a heated vat of waxy cherry-flavored coating. A pasty man in a windbreaker eyed Shana's ass. Jackpot glared at him.

"It has nothing to do with things falling my way," Jackpot said. "The woman, Bobbi, she told me that I had spunk."

"You know what *spunk* means in England?" Shana said.

"No."

"Come. It means come, jism," Shana said. She handed the coated cone to the man. He gave her the exact change: ninety-one cents. Shana shook the TIPS cup on the counter and yelled at him as he turned around to leave. "Thanks for the tip, cheapo! I hope you got a good look at my ass!" She began to wipe the droplets of the coating off the counter before they solidified.

"He did get a good look at your ass," Jackpot said.

"Everyone who gets a dipped cone gets a good look at my ass," Shana said. "Most tip me, though." She did a little shimmy.

"I'll call you tonight." Jackpot drove off westward on I-10, past Picacho Peak, to the small gray adobe house she shared with her mother. She skulked around the back through the greasy oleanders and the bamboo plants and climbed into her bedroom through the window.

Lisbiana was trying to make corn tamales for dinner that night, but Franky, the butter-eating midget who lived down the road, was chasing the goats in the yard with a yellow whiffle bat. Franky never spoke much and always had a stick of butter in his hand, always licking a stick of butter. Some said he was certifiably retarded; others said he was a misunderstood genius. Jackpot's mother said he was a pain in the ass. That evening she had to yell out her window six times before he stopped molesting the goats. Jackpot heard the hullabaloo from her bedroom in the back, nearly jumped out of her bed and chased him away herself. She hated Franky. He had once goosed her with his oily fingers in front of her friends, stained her white painter's pants. She belted him after the goosing, split his buttery lip. His face bunched up like a baby's, and he cried.

Jackpot knew she ought to help her mother in the kitchen, but she didn't feel like rolling out of bed just yet.

She studied the book club poster taped to the wall above her dresser: a puffy white kitten hanging from a branch by its forepaws. Shana had told Jackpot years ago that the cute and cuddly animals in the posters were all dead and stuffed.

"I doubt it," Jackpot had said. "The mouth is wet looking."

"They probably just sprayed it with water," Shana said. "That thing is as dead as a hamburger. Those eyes are marbles."

JACKPOT WALKED OUT to the kitchen. Lisbiana was sitting at the table, reading the paper. "That damn Franky," her mother said, wagging her head. "How long you been home?"

"Awhile," Jackpot said. "I got the job."

"I knew you would." Lisbiana folded the paper. "Which job?"

"For a woman. She's a Realtor. I mostly just answer her phone." Jackpot went to the cupboard and pulled out the box of Special K.

"No tamales? I made tamales."

"I'm not that hungry. Put them in the freezer." She grabbed a spoon and a bowl from the drying rack next to the sink. "I move Monday."

"Move?" Lisbiana said. Her black hair was up with one of Jackpot's plastic baby-doll barrettes. The eyebrows she had plucked years ago as a stripper had never grown back, and she hadn't bothered to draw them on today. Jackpot hated when her mother went around brow-free. It made her forehead look huge, abnormal.

"It's down in Tucson. That's part of the deal." She poured milk over the flakes.

"Are you sure this woman is okay? You should just work at the Dairy Cone with Shana. Nothing wrong with that."

"Dairy *Queen*," Jackpot said. "I'm only going to be there until August."

"Did you tell her that?"

"She didn't ask," Jackpot said. "It'll be perfect. I'll have enough for school in the fall, and I'll know Tucson much better."

"We'll see," Lisbiana said. "Don't you go buying your books for college yet." She flipped through the paper. "Did you see this story about the man in Phoenix who killed his two kids and then himself. Just awful."

"Just awful," Jackpot said.

THE PHONE PULSED as soon as she hung up. That was how it had been all morning. Bobbi was showing nineteen houses, the most yet, and her clients, both buyers and sellers, called constantly with questions. One lady needed to know how many gallons were in the pool at the Ventana Canyon house; another wanted the name of the plumbing contractor for a condo out in Marana. Jackpot couldn't answer any of them; she could only write them down and give them to Bobbi whenever she happened to dash in.

Mary Anne lay on the floor with her head at Jackpot's ankles. The pig always lingered in the office in the morning, nudging Jackpot's legs every few minutes, hoping to get a scratch. Jackpot did scratch her—her back was like a wool blanket, itchy and hispid, but pleasant to rub. That morning Jackpot pulled a tumid gray tick from the bristles behind Mary Anne's ear. She dropped it in an empty Diet Coke bottle and peeled off the Styrofoam label so she could watch it kick. It looked like a pinto bean. She would smash it outside on the driveway later.

She felt her own neck and head for ticks. The night before, Bobbi had blasted the swamp cooler—a moist, pervading chill was blown all through the house. In an effort to warm herself at two in the morning, she had climbed off her bed and spooned with Mary Anne, draping herself and the pig in all the blankets and sheets she had. She clung to the pig's back, wrapping her right arm and leg over her warm plumpness. Mary Anne was immaculate, much cleaner than a dog, and lots of people slept with their dogs.

At eleven or so, Mary Anne left the office to go do her business in the desert. She'd ordinarily return in the afternoon and watch *Love Connection* with Jackpot if things weren't too busy, but today Jackpot was tied up on the phone. No time to turn on the TV, no time for Chuck Woolery and L.A.'s glitziest and most desperate singles.

She started on the list of physicians, calling each of the six and talking their secretaries into renewing Bobbi's prescriptions for Valium. "Hello, this is Jacky Wilcox, and I'm calling for my boss, a patient of Dr. Bergman's. She needs her prescription refilled." Bobbi had warned Jackpot not to use her real name: "Some people aren't as accepting as me," she had said. "They may be put off by a girl named Jackpot." Each of the prescriptions was filled by a different pharmacist, so after all the calling, Jackpot had to spend a few hours driving around Tucson to pick them up. Even though it was June and 110 in the sun, she didn't mind. She wanted to get away from the damn phone, and driving through the pressing heat made her feel brave.

On her way out, she remembered the tick and went back to the desk to fetch it. She turned the bottle upside down and dumped it into her palm. She could feel its kicking legs brushing her skin like eyelashes.

Nick, the pool cleaner, was standing at the back of his

truck, untangling a vacuum hose. He came to Bobbi's every Monday and Thursday and tended to the pool. On Thursdays he also tended to Bobbi. Jackpot felt stupid when she first learned why Nick had marched up to Bobbi's room for the third Thursday in a row after he finished with the pool, why he was paid one hundred dollars a week for two short, twenty-minute pool cleanings, why Bobbi was always home on Thursday afternoons. The first time Bobbi called down to Jackpot, "Honey, will you send Nick up here to help me with my sink." The next week it was to move a dresser, and the third week it was to kill a scorpion. That last time, after the phone calmed down, Jackpot went up there to see the scorpion, and she heard Bobbi's carnal moans and squeals. From then on, Bobbi didn't bother with excuses; she'd just yell, "Send him up!"

Nick's truck was blocking Jackpot's brown Toyota compact. "You'll have to move that," she told him.

He was a tanned, leathery musclehead with frosted and feathered Bon Jovi hair and an arrowhead necklace. He never wore a shirt. "Make me," he said. He stood akimbo in front of Jackpot and flexed his pectorals: left, right, left, left, right.

"You're disgusting," she said.

"What's the problem? Do I make you hot?" He grinned stupidly, like a Hollywood chimp, exposing a chipped tooth.

"You make me sick. Now move that rattletrap." She dropped the tick on the hot driveway and stepped on it with her sandal. It popped and left a maroon circle on the cement.

"If you poke a pin in a fat tick's ass and let it run around, it will write your name in blood," Nick said.

"In your case it would write *asshole*."

"You're funny." He flipped his hair back. "We're having a party this weekend if you want to come," he said. "A trashed green car party."

"I don't think I'll be at your party." Jackpot eased into her ovenlike car, burning her legs on the vinyl. She rolled down the squeaky window, and Nick leaned his head in. She could smell the sweet tobacco on his breath.

"I'll leave directions on the desk in case you change your mind," he said.

"I won't," she said. "Now move your truck."

SHANA SAT ON the edge of the gushing whirlpool bath, soaking her Dairy Queen–weary feet, twirling the backing of her earring. She flipped through an oversize music and fashion magazine and gazed at a photograph of a kicky woman in platform sandals and hot pants. "You have it made," she said. "I'd be at the mall every day if I were you, JP."

"You get sick of it," Jackpot said. "Everything's too expensive anyway."

Mary Anne swaggered in and sat on the floor at Jackpot's feet, aiming her lard-filled teats at Shana. Jackpot scratched between Mary Anne's eyes. Mary Anne smacked her glistening lips in bliss.

"I don't get why that pig's in this nice house," Shana said.

"Bobbi likes her, I guess," Jackpot said. "She's cleaner than a dog. She's a glamour piggy."

"Fat as shit."

THAT AFTERNOON JACKPOT and Shana drove down to the nearly deserted shops by the university. At one athletic store that specialized in fraternity and sorority garb, Jackpot watched as Shana stuffed a seventy-dollar bathing suit down her shorts.

"Why should some sorority bitch have it?" Shana said when they stepped outside the store.

Jackpot thought about that. She couldn't figure out why some sorority bitch should have it.

THEY LOAFED BY Bobbi's pool, Shana modeling her new seventy-dollar suit, Jackpot still in her T-shirt and shorts. They sipped Diet Coke from fast-food plastic tumblers and ate a tray of gummy microwaved egg rolls as the radio blasted 96 Rock. The sun was almost down, but it was windy and still quite hot.

"You have it made," Shana said. She hummed along to an old Journey song: *Some will win, some will lose, some're born to sing the blues. . . .* "This sure beats Eloy."

"What have I missed in the last month?" Jackpot asked.

"Nothing much." Shana eased her way into the low end, then under. When she emerged, she snapped her hair back and said, "Franky's banned from Dairy Queen. Angela got a restraining order."

"Good," Jackpot said. "My mom should get one to keep the little fucker out of our yard."

"She should." Shana ducked under again.

IT TOOK THEM an hour to find the trashed green car party. The directions that Nick had scrawled were virtually indecipherable. His handwriting was like a jittery old woman's, and he spelled *hospital:* h-o-s-b-i-d-l-e. At the bottom of a hill on Calle Barcelona, they saw ten or so cars parked in the dirt shoulder. They pulled last in line and hiked down the sandy arroyo, Jackpot pausing every few minutes to shake pebbles from her sandals.

"There's the trashed green car," Shana said. A bit of chrome from the gnarled fender reflected the moonlight. Some guys, most of whom looked like Nick, were sitting on the hood drinking beer from plastic cups and earnestly rocking their heads to corrosive speed metal. "At least they have a keg."

"At least," Jackpot said. She hadn't wanted to go to the trashed green car party, but Shana had insisted they go when she found the directions on Jackpot's desk and heard about the relationship between Nick and Bobbi. She wanted to see this Nick, wanted to see why Bobbi paid him so well.

He loped up to them from behind a rogue olive tree. "If you want beer, I need two bucks from each of you." He stared at Shana's breasts. They pushed against the rubber iron-on of Darth Vader that emblazoned her mini-T. She stared at his breasts. His were bigger.

"I'll pay for both of us," Jackpot said. She handed Nick a crumpled five from her purse.

"Keg's back behind the trashed green car," he said, motioning with his head. Jackpot noticed that he must have brushed his hair for the party. It looked fluffier than usual, and the part in the middle was exact, fighting against the chipped tooth for facial symmetry. He walked back behind the olive tree, and they heard girlish giggles.

"He would be cute if he cut his hair," Shana said.

"No."

"Well, I can see why someone like Bobbi gives him one hundred a week."

"No," Jackpot repeated.

SHANA GOT DRUNK quickly, standing in the dirt by the keg and refilling her cup. She met everyone that way—everyone visited the keg. Jackpot stood beside her, nursing the same warm Coors the whole time and trying to look as absent as possible. Shana talked to them all: nearly twenty different guys and two girls. As soon as they'd shoot their cups full and walk away from the keg, Shana would turn to Jackpot with her analysis: dork, inbred, slut, cute for a complete loser. Jackpot mostly agreed, but she quickly grew weary of the game, wanted to go home. "No way," Shana said. "Maybe when the keg's dry."

"I know where we can buy more if that's what you want," Jackpot said.

"Oh please," Shana said. "Give me a break." She sauntered off toward the trashed green car, swaying her Daisy Dukes and howling—whooping it up. She sat on the hood next to Nick, who had returned from behind the olive tree with his doughy rock-video girlfriend.

Jackpot dumped the remaining few drops of her watery beer and sat down in the dirt. It was still hot, and she wiped the sweat from her upper lip. When she looked up at the trashed green car, Shana and Nick were gone, the girlfriend was sitting by herself, swaying drunkenly.

"IT WASN'T AS BIG as I thought," Shana reported on the way back to Bobbi's. "I mean, you'd think for a hundred dollars—"

"I really don't want to hear about it," Jackpot said.

"At least I didn't have to pay for it."

"At least," Jackpot said.

A few minutes later, Jackpot pulled over at a minimart to let Shana puke.

BOBBI HAD GIVEN Jackpot a checklist of people to call: the caterer, the country-swing band, the company that rented tents and chairs, another that rented a stage, and another that rented ponies. Between the hoedown organizing and doing her routine work, Jackpot didn't have much time for Mary Anne, only a quick scratch here and there.

As the event loomed closer, Jackpot felt a nervous hollow in her stomach. She double-checked with the caterers and the pony people, logged everything in a small notebook. She resented Nick—he really worked only an hour a week—but then she imagined Bobbi naked, everything sagging and wrinkled and discolored. She decided that he earned his check.

Lately he'd been digging a deep barbecue pit in the hardened dirt behind the pool area. On that Thursday, Bobbi watched him from her balcony and yelled "Looking good!" a few times, loudly enough for Jackpot to hear from the desk. When he walked by Jackpot on his way to Bobbi, sweat rolled off his ripples, and drops the size of quarters spattered the Mexican tiles.

"Can't you at least towel off before you come in here and stink everything up?" Jackpot said.

"That's not what Bobbi wants." Nick leaned over the desk. Bigger drops of his sweat tapped loose papers. He smelled like the goats at home. "What about you?"

"What about me?" Jackpot curled her lip in disgust. It snagged on her dry teeth.

"I think if you came and watched me dance, you'd change your attitude real quick," he said.

"Dance?"

"At the Showboat. Monday's ladies' night."

"I'd rather not," she said. "Now get off the desk. You're messing it up."

BOBBI HAD CLEARED her schedule so that she could be home for the two days immediately preceding the hoedown. She scurried around, generating nervous energy in Jackpot.

Bobbi was scrubbing everything in the house that could stand it, and the whole place reeked of artificial pine. "You have to call my doctors today. My pills are running out," she told Jackpot as she darted by the desk with a bucket and yellow rubber gloves pulled up past her elbows. "Don't forget."

The next time she ran by, she stopped in the doorway and asked, "Where the hell is Nick? He was supposed to get the coals just right in the pit. They're not just right."

"I haven't seen him yet," Jackpot said.

"I'll do it myself," Bobbi said. "As usual. Come out and help me with the logs."

They walked out into the heat and looked into the pit. At the bottom, about six feet down, were heaps of smoldering mesquite embers, gray and white. Jackpot savored the smoke—just like Agua Prieta. When she was younger, she and her mother drove down there to visit her two aunts. The whole town had smelled of burning mesquite. It was the only redeeming quality of Agua Prieta, the town where each of the inhabitants, including Jackpot's aunts, bargained for everything all the time. One of her aunts, Marta, had offered Jackpot, who was only ten at the time, a mangy puppy in exchange for her hair. Jackpot's mother wouldn't acquiesce, even when Marta told them that the puppy would be killed when it got bigger, ground up and rolled into chimichangas for the gringos. When Jackpot was sixteen, she got a Peter Pan cut and mailed her three-foot braids to Marta. She hadn't asked for anything in return, but Marta mailed her a crappy one-eyed doll. The doll did smell of mesquite, though.

"WE NEED TWICE as much down there," Bobbi said, rabidly twitching her face. "That goddamn Nick! Where the hell is he? None of the branches are even cut yet." She kicked the tangled mound of mesquite sticks with her nuclear white Ked.

"We can do it," Jackpot said. "Or I can do it, if you have something else you want to do."

"No. I'll do it." She lifted the ax. The twinkles on her nails caught the sun and flashed like sparklers. "You go back inside and watch that phone. Come get me if the tent guy calls."

Jackpot passed Nick as she walked back into the house. "She's pissed," she told him.

"What for?"

She ignored him and sat down at the desk. Mary Anne was sprawled on the cool tiles at her feet, snoring lightly. Jackpot reached down and gave her a scratch under the chin. "Good piggy," she said. She gazed wearily at the hypnotizing ceiling fan and waited for the phone to ring.

ABOUT AN HOUR LATER, Bobbi, red-flushed with streaks of makeup coursing down her neck, walked in, clucked her tongue, and screamed, "Sooey! Sooey! Sooeeey!"

Mary Anne perked her ears and struggled up, hooves frantically slipping this way and that on the tiles. She walked over to Bobbi. Bobbi looked over to Jackpot. "Have you called my doctors yet? I'm going to need you to go pick up my prescriptions tomorrow morning."

"I'll call now," Jackpot said. She started down the list, ticking the doctors' names after the arrangements were made with the secretaries. She had a problem with Dr. Martin's secretary. She told Jackpot that Bobbi needed to come in for blood work before the doctor could okay another refill. "I'll check with Bobbi," Jackpot said. "Can you hold on one second?"

She walked out back and looked to the pit where Bobbi, Mary Anne, and Nick were standing. Nick raised the ax over his head and brought the blunt side down on Mary Anne's neck with a meaty thwack. Mary Anne tried to step away, fell sideways, and squealed. "Hit her again! Hit her right!" Bobbi demanded. He hit her again. This time Jackpot heard a moist crunch. "Now string her up."

Jackpot stepped back inside and picked up the phone. She stared at the receiver for a few seconds, then she blankly spoke to the secretary: "Bobbi says she'll just get it from the other five doctors she has who prescribe it to her."

She walked upstairs and pulled her suitcase out from under the bed. She could hear the phone ringing down at her desk, but she didn't stop packing until she was done. She hefted her suitcase down the stairs and out the door. Bobbi ran up to her in the driveway.

"What's this all about?" She had a splatter of Mary Anne's brown blood on her shoulder. Almost all of her makeup had melted away, and her eyes looked smaller, like they had been sucked deeper into her head.

"I'm leaving." Jackpot shoved her suitcase into the passenger seat. "I quit."

"Leaving me in the lurch two days before my barbecue hoedown? Please!" Bobbi whined, pressing her palms on her cheeks. "What is this? I don't understand."

"I'm leaving you in the lurch two days before your barbecue hoedown." Jackpot sat down and started her car.

Bobbi screamed, "Jackpot!"

JACKPOT PULLED OFF I-10 at the second Eloy exit, the one flanked with fast-food huts and cheap trucker motels. The air-conditioning in her Toyota had died at the end of Bobbi's street, so her windows were rolled down, and her back was drenched with sweat against the seat. She hadn't wanted to return home—she knew her mother would be smug about the whole thing—but she couldn't afford to pay rent somewhere in Tucson—not yet. A five-mile stretch connected the businesses to the real Eloy. This stretch ran through dusty cotton fields, nothing else.

She passed Franky waddling along the road. He looked at her with beseeching eyes and stuck out his tiny thumb. Not a chance, she thought, and she looked away. Then she stopped and threw her car in reverse. "Get in," she told him. "It's too hot for me to leave someone out here—even you."

He swung the door open and climbed in. His little feet kicked over the edge of the seat. He wore children's Velcro sneakers, butter-stained work pants, and a V-necked T-shirt that showed the thick black hair on his miniature, boxy chest. He had no butter with him. "You have pretty eyes," Franky told Jackpot.

Jackpot stared intently at the faded yellow highway line as she sped toward her house.

As they drove by the school and Shana's place, Franky leaned over the stick shift and grabbed Jackpot's crotch. She looked down: chubby cocktail-wiener fingers and dimpled knuckles. She calmly (was even whistling) pulled the car onto the dirt shoulder. "What are you doing?" she asked.

"Looking for change," Franky snorted.

She cuffed him in the ear. Hard. "Get out," she said. "Get out now."

Franky rubbed his ear and got out. Jackpot made a U-turn toward Dairy Queen. She figured one month of dipping cones wouldn't kill her.

bears, bikes,

CAMPING ON THE HILL wasn't that bad except for the stories of Sugar, the demented, fat brown bear who had supposedly raped a girl in '85 and harassed campers of both genders all the time. I'd seen Sugar the summer before; he was in town one night picking through the trash behind Athena's, the Greek restaurant where I worked each summer. He did seem crazy: Cookie-Monster wiggly eyes dancing in the lights, and hips—big wide eunuch hips. Many women in Telluride would look out their bathroom windows at night to find Sugar peering in at them, drooling, with one paw moving around down at his private parts. He smeared his wet nose prints on windows all over town and left other evidence, too. A waitress at Petey's café swears that Sugar stole her bras and panties right off her clothesline and left everything else untouched.

When I finally left for the hill, I think there were eight people sleeping on Jana's floor; and a dog, a Frisbee-crazed mutt named Dylan, who licked my neck all night while I slept next to him under the kitchen table. It wasn't fair that Jana had to open her place for all the wayward summer people, everyone who went up there and worked scrub-jobs for a few hours a day so they could spend the rest of their time smoking pot or hang-gliding or making jewelry or hiking or whatever. The eight of us were sprawled all over, some couples coupling, plus sleeping bags and packs and wafts of foot odor like old cheese. Nowhere to walk. I had to go camp on the hill.

THE SUMMER BEFORE, my friend Ubi and I scored a great place to live: a basement with a little kitchen for only $250 a month. The owner was a Manhattan escapee who did way too many drugs to efficiently run the third-rate pizza place he had in town. He was always sniffing, and his face was a constant ruddy flush. I swear he never even set foot in that basement. I think we only paid for June, and he didn't bother us at all for the rest of the summer. Too bad he moved out of town at the end of that summer when his restaurant finally went under. The woman who bought his house wasn't renting out the basement. I checked.

Ubi and I challenged each other way too much on our bikes that summer. No one else would go riding with us. We'd fly down trails so fast that it felt like our brains were being pushed and rattled into the back of our skulls, like our faces would peel off. I spent half of that summer with a hand-sized Christmas scab, green and red, on the side of my face. Ubi broke his collarbone. It was kind of my fault.

"Just go," I said. "I'm sure it's been done. There are tire tracks on that third ledge. If you won't, I will."

He went, hopping and skidding and clanking down, actually making it about halfway past the series of boulder drop-offs, until he leaned out instead of in and swan-dived into a little aspen. His bike wound up propped neatly against a stump, like he had parked it there. When he picked up a rock to throw at me, he realized his collarbone was broken, and he cursed me instead. It was okay. He was still allowed to bus tables at Petey's, and his sling elicited good tips and a lot more help from the waitresses.

It had been kind of a weird summer—Ubi and I had the same girlfriend, Erica, for about three weeks. It's not as if the three of us were in bed at the same time, it wasn't like that, but it was still pretty odd. She came down from Steamboat Springs and had no place to stay, so we let her live with us in the basement. How could we have said no to her caramel-colored hair and that perfect bean-shaped mole sitting on her cheek? How could we have sent her to the hill to be attacked by Sugar? There was no way. Her bike was savory, too—although she couldn't ride for shit. Some nights she'd be in my bed, other nights she'd be in Ubi's, and Ubi and I would bum condoms off of each other. We never really talked about it, Ubi and I. There were none of those jealousy games, at least not until she left.

One night when I got back from work, Ubi was sitting on the kitchen counter holding a note from her: *Thanks for letting me stay here. Love, Erica.*

"Maybe if you did the dishes and didn't leave your shit all over the place, she wouldn't have left," Ubi said to me.

"Fuck you," I said.

"No, fuck you."

"Maybe if you washed your hair and practiced some personal hygiene, she still might be here," I told him. "Try brushing that yellow crud off your teeth every once in a while. People might be able to talk to you without puking."

He threw a plate of dried spaghetti at me, and I tackled him. We beat the shit out of each other pretty good—two bloody noses, a busted lip, and a fork wound in the thigh— but the next morning, we went on an awesome ride up past the falls and forgot the whole thing.

UBI WASN'T UP there yet when I left Jana's floor and went to camp on the hill. His school didn't let out until the middle of June, and I was done in early May. He was in smoggy Pasadena, and I was in D.C., so all year we'd look forward to the summers up there in Telluride, the town squeezed so snugly between giant peaks that only half of it got any sun during the day. Neither of us could stand the heat of our hometown, Tucson, during the summer, so we went straight from school to Telluride. For me that meant flying into Denver and sitting on buses for hours. Ubi just drove his old Volvo station wagon from Caltech straight on through.

Every time I went up there to Telluride, it took me about a week before the sickening grin of amazement left my face. I'd walk around on the first day just staring and smiling, probably with my mouth open like a retard's. The mountains were in your face, precariously lumbering up to the sky, and looking as if they could fold in on the town whenever they felt like it. Always snow-capped, always freshly snow-capped, even in July, and sharply pointed like Indian arrowheads.

I spent the next week or so searching for places to live and shit, and waiting for Ubi. It wasn't until the third or fourth day of hill-living that I found a secret bathroom near the fire station that was always clean and always had toilet paper. Unfortunately, it only lasted a few days. A band of scummy patchouli-stinking hippies found it and virtually moved in. They were the types who followed the Dead and panhandled in every city along the way, even though they all probably went to Brown or Duke and drove new Saabs with new kayaks and mountain bikes racked to the top.

"IT'S $650 PER MONTH, water and gas included, and I need a security deposit of $200. You do have a job?" She was a real estate agent, lots of orange lipstick and a mouth that could hold a fist—one of the hordes of agents who moved up there in hopes of selling land to Cher and the like. I handed her my driver's license, and she handed me the keys to go check it out.

As soon as I got the front door unlocked, I ran in and used the bathroom. It was only a one-bedroom apartment, big though, either a time-share or a vacation rental during the ski season.

The Realtor-hag said she'd only allow one or two people to live in the place, but I knew, with its big living room, that it could comfortably sleep six or eight. Rent would be around a hundred each. I just had to wait for Ubi and ask around up on the hill for other people who wanted to go in on it.

I ran into Sally outside the real estate office after I returned the keys. She was wearing one of those placards that advertised the lunch special at Petey's—black bean chili and cornbread, $3.99—and was ringing a bell. The only parts of Sally that fit her little-girl name were her hands. Tiny hands. Like they stopped growing when she was six years old playing with her Easy-Bake Oven. She was a rockclimber and a member of the Monkey Chow group, who liked me because I gave her a great deal on a rope and some carabiners a few summers before.

The Monkey Chow group would leave Telluride for Joshua Tree in August, and stop in Flagstaff at the Ralston-Purina factory to load up on Monkey Chow. They ate only Monkey Chow and drank only water for six or so weeks while they camped and climbed. They were kind of conceited—like they knew they were legendary. I had seen a few of them up on the hill, and I asked Sally if any of them needed a place.

"Definitely Stu and Dave would go in on it," she said.

"Great."

"Hey, weren't you the one who used to talk about Sugar all the time last summer?"

"Yeah, I guess that was me," I said.

"Well, I saw him the other night. He had his head in someone's car out near the racquet club. I don't know what they left in that car, but he sure wanted it. He was trying to squeeze his fat ass through that window."

"They probably left a *Playboy* in the car."

THE OWNER OF Athena's restaurant was Camille, a fleshy Italian woman who thought she was everyone's mother. Actually, she couldn't even control her own boy-crazy daughter and bong-crazy son. She didn't like to hire hill-sleepers. "They're messy, late, and they stink," she said. I kept my hill-sleeping a secret.

I was clean. I took showers at the town park for fifty cents and washed away the smell of wet grass and pine sap. The water was bone-cracking cold, so cold that a three-minute shower required a two-hour nap to recover from the energy lost to shivering.

Camille liked me for some reason. I was one of the few workers who wouldn't show up high every shift. The cooks were the worst. Always fried. Pupils dilated to black pucks, and stupid, wondrous grins.

One night during the bluegrass festival, when everyone from real hillbillies to Denver lawyers swarmed into town, it took the cooks more than two hours to make some scrambled eggs for a couple from West Virginia. Scrambled eggs for dinner is pretty weird, but still, two hours. Everyone was waiting tables that night, even Stretch and Elmo, the dishwashers, who could barely speak. The trick was to take an order and look in the back to see if anything close to it came up. If it did, you had to take it immediately and hope the customers or the other people waiting tables didn't complain. Every thirty minutes or so, the cooks would scream that there were no clean dishes, so some of us would run back there and spray off a few. Sometimes, if the order was just a sandwich or some hummus and falafel, I'd go back there and prepare it myself.

I made over a hundred bucks in tips each of those bluegrass nights, but I worked my ass off. I knew Ubi'd be pissed again that he missed the bluegrass and all the money that came with it. It was good that the festival happened in the beginning of the summer. It gave me a financial kick that let me coast for the rest of the summer.

I was so exhausted that I didn't mind the hill in the slightest. As soon as I got up there, I'd unroll my sleeping bag and plop down in the wet grass, not once worrying about waking up to Sugar mauling me. I would wake up to the sun, and most of the time with a mouth full of weeds and leaves, and frozen drool on my cheek.

. . .

I RODE A LOT during the day, even though Ubi wasn't up there yet. It wasn't that exciting. It was good, but not that exciting. All the rest of the year, pedaling through the over-stomped and illegal trails of Glover Park in D.C., I'd look forward to Telluride, where the trails are endless and you don't get accosted by sneaky urban rangers named Betty J who threaten to confiscate your bike and slap you with a fifty-dollar fine. Still, without Ubi there to dare, it was different. I used my brakes more and didn't acquire many good scabs.

New houses stretched west toward Saw Pit, big faux-rustic houses, the kind that remain empty all year except in September during the film festival or a few weeks in winter for skiing. They hadn't been there the year before, none of them. There was a new stoplight too, right in front of the hardware store.

Ralph Lauren has a ranch up near there. He spent millions redoing the fence that holds in his glamour cattle because it didn't look weathered enough. Once, on our way to Montrose, Ubi and I stopped and pissed on that fence and threw rocks at his fashion cows, too. The Double RL. What an asshole.

I shouldn't say that. Later that same day, while I was deliberating in the supermarket in Montrose whether or not I should spend four dollars on a box of Frankenberry, I realized that if I were as rich as Ralph Lauren, I'd have the same ranch in the same exact location. On our way back to Telluride, we didn't stop to piss on his fence or throw rocks at his cows.

THE LAST NIGHT of the bluegrass, the restaurant was chaos. The three cooks got in a fight, and two left. Maria, who fancied herself the best waitress in the place, dropped a moth-erload of food and dishes and started to cry. Camille cried too and left. Just walked out of her own restaurant. None of the wait staff left. We all needed the money, and customers were lined up outside the door.

I ran into a guy from Tucson—Brad. He went to my high school, and we used to call him Bug-Boy because he made a nervous clicking noise like a cicada. We tortured the hell out of him. I almost did it, I almost called him Bug-Boy that night, but at the last second, I remembered his name. "Hey, Brad," I said.

"Mulligan, what're you doing up here?" He was pleasant, even though if I had been him and him me, I would've kicked my ass. I'd been awful to the poor guy for four years, and there I was busing his table and serving him water and bread.

"Just this and riding my bike," I told him loudly. He used to wear a hearing aid, but I couldn't see it that night in the restaurant.

It turned out that Bug-Boy's dad owned a huge house on the sunny side of town. Bug-Boy was up there for a few days, and then it was back to Tucson. He left a pretty good tip. I don't know what they were serving in the cafeteria at his col-lege, but he turned out to be a regular musclehead. He could've easily kicked my ass. He should've.

Once, in tenth grade, Ubi and I convinced Bug-Boy to go up onstage at school during the science fair awards assembly.

"Congratulations!" Ubi slapped his back.

"Go on up and get your award," I told him.

Poor Bug-Boy went up there, grinning like a baby, ready to receive his plaque. We had lied to him, though. They hadn't announced his name. The principal looked confused at Bug-Boy's arrival onstage, and he whispered something to him. Bug-Boy turned red and ran out of the assembly. I felt shitty, but of course Ubi laughed like hell.

WITH CAMILLE GONE, we all started making ourselves at home behind the bar. The counter next to the sink in the kitchen was crammed with our jumbo experimental cocktails. Charity, a round-faced and wild-eyed waitress—a hell of a mountain biker—was getting me drunk and pinching my ass. "I made this especially for you, Mulligan, you look like you could use it." It was a brown drink, thick and syrupy, like dirty motor oil—probably just Kahlúa or something. The booze made the night speed. I told crude jokes about inbred West Virginians to customers and ate anything I could get my hands on in the kitchen. No one got out of the place until after three, and we left it a mess.

Charity got me down to the river. I soaked my feet in the ice water, and she dove right in. She looked too good, too carefree, out there splashing around in the moonlight, so I scooped up a mudball and nailed her in the head. "You're dead!" she yelled. We mud-wrestled for a while, grinding glop into each other's hair, both exhausted from waiting tables, but nonetheless expending everything we had. I bet Sugar was nearby, watching as Charity finger-painted circles and stars in the cold mud that coated my back.

Ubi had rolled into town that night. I saw his trashed Volvo out in front of Jana's as I skulked back to the hill. I was too tired to greet him then. I plopped down, pretty much still covered in mud, using just my sleeping bag as a pillow. There was a freaky, warm wind on the hill that night, not like the blow-dryer desert winds in Tucson, but one that calmly pushed me into sleep.

. . .

HIS HAIR WAS down past his shoulders, stringy, greasy, and dyed ink-black. He was kind of scary in that morning sun— I didn't know who the hell he was at first. He was pale, and his face was sunken in, like a Munster or a member of the Addams Family, only his clothes, a buckskin shirt and green wool pants, looked like something Davy Crockett would've worn.

"Do you have that eighty bucks you owe me?" was the first thing Ubi said when he found me up on the hill.

Ubi had a girl with him, also tragically ghoulish, with a big floppy velvet hat and blue circles around her eyes like a deranged harlequin. All she did was giggle and burrow her head into his shoulder and back. I wondered where he had found her. Not at Caltech; she looked too stupid.

"Where's your bike?" I asked.

"Sold it. Look, do you have the money?"

It was wet and muddy and hard to get out of my pocket, but I gave it to him. "Brad's up here," I told him. "Bug-Boy."

Ubi snickered.

He had no interest in the place I found and no interest in staying in Telluride. He was headed to the Four Corners because it was mystical there. He thought he was a shaman, and he needed to go to the spiritual lands of northwestern New Mexico. I instantly had enough of his Jim Morrison crap, so I was almost glad when he and the clown-girl left town. I kept thinking about his bike: a dreamy hand-built titanium frame with front and rear suspension, all for two ounces under twenty-three pounds. He probably traded it for a kukumaka stick or some magic beans. I had spent four hours with him one night the summer before building the back wheel, spoke by spoke, talking about where we were going to ride the next day.

. . .

WHEN I WENT back to the real estate place, the big-mouthed woman told me the place was rented. "You snooze, you lose," she said.

"Clever," I said.

Sally told me later that the Monkey Chowers were leaving in July anyway.

There was a problem with hill-sleeping that night: skunks. Two people, some guys from Australia, had been sprayed, and the whole hill was unbearably pungent. The skunks didn't smell natural. They smelled like burning tires.

The screen door to Jana's place was open, and there were already about five people on the floor when I got there. I took my spot under the table for a night of Dylan's Alpo kisses.

CHARITY FOUND ME the next morning and shook me awake. "Get up, you lazy piece of shit, and let's go riding."

We rode the Bear Creek Trail, which was mostly just single-track switchbacks that wound up the ski slopes. She kicked my ass. From the start, she plugged ahead and soon was out of my sight. At the top she let me have it.

"You're pathetic" was how she put it. "I've been waiting up here for twenty minutes. I thought you were supposed to be good. Last summer you and Ubi were supposed to be the best." She laughed at me.

I was about to puke, breathing like an old lady smoker. I guess I hadn't really adjusted to the altitude yet.

She wasted me downhill, too. I don't know what she had for breakfast, but it gave her an ungodly amount of energy and took away her fear. She was out of my sight in seconds and didn't even wait for me at the bottom.

That night the restaurant was mellow. I was glad that Charity wasn't working because she would have just teased the hell out of me—I deserved it. Mostly just locals came in, except for a family from New York who took about an hour to decide what they wanted from our very limited menu. Bug-Boy came in again. He was going back to Tucson in the morning. Driving straight through, about twelve hours.

Some guys from the bike shop left an interesting tip: a little bag of 'shrooms, mostly caps—about half a handful. I didn't think the waitress, Maria, deserved them. She didn't. She was a lousy waitress—grumpy and forgetful. I was always picking up her slack, apologizing for her attitude. So I ate the 'shrooms right there, crunching them to dusty grit and washing them down with half a glass of warm, flat beer. I wanted something to happen.

Things became funny, and the ugly patterned carpeting looked interesting squirming around. I had to try for it. I had to work at it, concentrate: the carpet will swirl, the walls will throb, green and red will take on new meanings. I focused hard, but I soon realized that the pathetic 'shrooms had nothing to do with it. The carpet wasn't really squirming, and nothing was really funny.

Up on the hill, which still smelled like skunks, I looked at the few lights of the town and moved my head around. No tracers. Really all I got were dirt-flavored burps and a stomachache. Shitty 'shrooms. I couldn't sleep either, so I jogged down the hill.

I walked around the sleeping town. It looked like Disneyland on a rainy day: clean, quaint, and deserted. I wondered when a McDonald's would move in. Probably soon. Not one with big golden arches. It'd be more subdued—decorated Santa Fe style with turquoise and pink trim and old Western artifacts, like spurs and wagon wheels, on its walls.

Over near the condos where Jana lived, I saw Sugar under a floodlight, digging through a Dumpster. He found a shit-smeared Pamper and bounded off to the trees with it in his mouth like it was a prize. It was his prize.

I unrolled my sleeping bag next to Bug-Boy's truck in the driveway of his dad's huge house. I wanted to ride with him back to Tucson—the oven—if he'd let me.

cul-de-sacs

TAKING EVERYONE TO THE Pima Air Museum was a mean idea, I admit. The only other people I remember seeing there that afternoon were four German tourists in fluorescent, synthetic sweatsuits and a few gossiping senior-citizen volunteers hiding from the white sun under a fiberglass ramada. The museum sits in a corner of the Boneyard, a vast dumping ground for spent military aircraft: miles of expired planes, helicopters, and jets, baking and disintegrating in the sun. The actual museum, an echoey old air force hangar filled with the thick smell of corn dogs and popcorn from the snack bar, is home to hundreds of boring seventies exhibits like *Blacks in Uniform* and *Historic Propellers*. But I didn't want to sit around the house all day while Ann and Clarissa went to the mall like they had every Saturday so far that summer; that's why I insisted we all get in the car and drive out to the dead planes.

We spent most of our time on the rock-lined walkways that wound through a group of fifty or so rotting, fading aircraft in the dirt outside the hangar. We had prepared for the sun with hats and UV-blocking sunglasses, and we were smeared with waxy SPF 45 sunscreen. We smelled tropical. Out there in the aircraft graveyard, our antisun measures didn't seem to help, though. I could feel the rays pressing down, sizzling through it all. We stopped at each plane and sat in the shade of one of its wings—if it still had its wings. I'd examine the rivets, peek into the cockpit if possible, and exaggerate my interest in the aerodynamics. Under one, I read aloud from the brochure: "The Convair B-58 Hustler was the first supersonic bomber in history capable of delivering nuclear bombs. . . ." Ann pretended to listen to what I was reading. Clarissa sighed loudly and lifted her hair off the back of her neck. My son, Martin, didn't do anything because at that point he was asleep in his stroller, hiding under his ball cap.

Some of the jets were amazingly massive, bigger than strip malls, with windows and engines still intact. Most looked too big to fly, like it was wrong that things that big ever flew. The wheels on the landing gear of some were taller than me with Martin on my shoulders.

"It scares me to think that maybe only one guy was controlling this thing as it hurtled through the sky," I said, gazing up into the greasy shocks and axles of a carrier, one of the last we looked at.

"Can we leave?" Clarissa said. "I'm thirsty."

"This is torture," Ann finally said, pinching her temples like the heat had given her a migraine.

I was keeping Ann and Clarissa in the blasting sun, draining energy from them, making them too tired and grumpy to go off together later on.

"UNCLE ED, that place sucked," Clarissa told me on the way home. "And aim one of those vents over here." She was in the backseat, out of the air conditioner's range. Sweat trailed down her neck and dragged some of her makeup with it. I adjusted the vent on the right, directing it toward her, knowing that the cooled air would never reach her.

"I'll think of something better for next time," I told her. That following weekend, I tried to come up with somewhere as hot and as boring to visit, but not too obviously so. I couldn't. They went off to the mall.

CLARISSA HAD COME to stay with us for the summer. She's my older brother's daughter, and that spring she hadn't been able to get along with him. She was eighteen then, headed to Carleton College in Minnesota that fall. Smart, lazy as hell, and with her honey-colored hair and showgirl legs, attractive in an obvious way. It was her job to take care of Martin and clean the house while Ann and I worked, but all she did was stick Martin in his playpen, lounge around, and watch talk shows. When I'd get home from work, she'd be draped on the couch, asleep, her hair spilled all over the cushions—the TV blaring and snack-food wrappers and crumbs scattered on the floor in front of her. Martin would also be asleep because he'd stayed up late, making Ann and me tired. The thing that really got me was that Ann didn't care that Clarissa was a slacker milking us for five dollars an hour plus free room and board. She liked Clarissa—probably because she didn't get along with any of her coworkers at the bank: "They huddle around *Days of Our Lives* in the lounge from twelve to one every day, and then when they come back out front, all they ever want to talk about is that damn show. And they all wear too much perfume."

Toward the end of June, I'd sneak up to sleeping Clarissa if I returned home before Ann and slam my briefcase down on the coffee table, or I'd pant primitively in her ear. She'd wake up and cuss at me and complain to Ann about it when Ann got home.

Once, when Clarissa left a half-eaten hot dog on the arm of the couch, I plucked it from its ketchupy bun and slipped it into her hand. I watched as she squeezed the meaty insides out of the casing and onto herself. Then I woke her up by grunting loudly.

"What the hell?" she moaned.

"Interesting dream you were having," I told her.

"What?" she said, sitting up, looking at the mess in her hand. She was confused only for a second.

"You had quite a grip on that wiener."

"You're vile," she said, throwing the hot dog at me.

Then Ann got home, and the two of them went out as usual, leaving me with Martin, who had almost mastered escaping from his playpen. Despite what the pediatrician said about his slower-than-normal, eleventh-percentile verbal development—which shot up to the fifty-second percentile the fall after Clarissa left—Martin was a great two-year-old. Not fussy, not gassy, not wild, and ninety percent toilet-trained. I think he hated Clarissa, too—at least I fantasized that he hated her. We bonded in this hate.

Each night after Ann and Clarissa left and I calmed down, Martin and I went about our routines. I'd slip on my running shoes and strap Martin in his stroller, and off we'd go. I got to know our neighbors that summer. I learned everybody's business. There were only three houses in our cul-de-sac—including ours.

We all lived in model houses for a development that had flopped, gone bankrupt. These homes were priced to move, and because Ann and I thought back then that we'd like to have a few more kids, we couldn't refuse. Four bedrooms and a two-car garage. The homes were big, and all three looked exactly alike: sand-colored stucco, red Mexican-tile roofs, natural desert xeriscaping in the front, and backyards with peanut-shaped pools enclosed by black wrought-iron fences. I could've walked into the neighbors' house across the street and known right where to find their bathrooms and linen closets.

I wouldn't have done that. The man across the street was a dentist who looked exactly like Rex Morgan, M.D., from the comics page: stiff, ink-black hair and pronounced, handsome-guy cheekbones. His wife wore baggy, loose clothes and big ceramic beads and spoke with what I always thought was a bogus British accent. She claimed she had worked with Jane Goodall and had a Ph.D. in primate zoology, but I doubted it. They had a pet chimp that she couldn't control. "He's not a pet," she'd say each time she came over to our place to fetch him. "He's been socialized with humans and thinks he's our child. We treat him as such."

Every month when Ann got her period, the chimp would be pounding on our back door, scratching his nails on the screen, showing his yellow fangs, and twisting his pink crayon dick—and screaming and shrieking. He was big, bigger than you'd think a chimp was, with thick linebacker shoulders and feet he could fist-up and punch with. When he was all sexed up, he was not the least bit cute. I'd go upstairs, lean out the bathroom window, and dump pans of cold water on him, refilling from the bathtub faucet. But he wouldn't retreat until his owners came over and calmed him down with a green liquid they'd spray from a perfume atomizer.

They were allowed to keep him because our neighborhood was outside the Tucson city limits. I only knew their last name: Rombough. I called them Chimp People. Their chimp I called Romboner.

To the west of us was a hardy Mormon family of nine giant girls and their giant parents. All the girls had blond, braided hair and wore frilly dresses and knee-high socks. Swiss Misses of the Sonora Desert. You couldn't tell them apart from one another. Martin called them all Nan because Nan was the one who first baby-sat him—plus Nan was the only thing he could say anyway. His bottle he called Nan, me he called Nan, Ann he called Nan. The Mormon girls had all been good baby-sitters: they held Martin and always cleaned the house before we got home. I still don't know why we kept Clarissa on. I should have sent her home to my brother after the first week and had the Swiss Misses baby-sit all summer.

The Swiss Misses never fought, and when they swam, they wore those old-lady-type, skirted swimsuits and rubber, flower-covered bathing caps. They'd wave to Martin and me from their pool through the twists of wrought iron. We'd wave back and stroll on.

The Chimp People were a little more interesting. Each night the woman, clad in rudely colored spandex, would do step aerobics or Jazzercise in the living room, and Romboner would sit in the window and clap his long, wrinkled hands. When the dentist got home, he'd kiss the chimp first, then his sweaty wife. Martin and I frequently witnessed this through their ten-by-fourteen picture window. We had that same window at home.

Because the housing development never developed, desolate paved streets with low hills sprawled for miles into the desert. Some teenagers from town would cruise them and leave their crunched beer cans and condom wrappers, but otherwise no one ever went out there. The city planners didn't bother naming any of the streets, not even ours. According to the U.S. Postal Service, we lived on Route 67G, but there were no street signs. That made it difficult to give people directions to our house. If anyone got lost out on those streets, it might've been hours before they got back to civilization. It was a labyrinth of identically barren cul-de-sacs and confusing, curving roads. The development was going to be called Blue Canyons. There were no blue canyons out there. No canyons of any color.

I never got lost pushing Martin in his stroller. We stuck to the same four streets—a three-mile loop with two turn-offs. We'd see mangy coyotes loping through the scrub, nervous jackrabbits, and once in a while, a gila monster. Snakes, even rattlers, would lie in the streets in the early evening, warming their bellies on the asphalt. Along the way, I'd pull the orange-vinyl surveyor flags from bushes and stakes and tie them to the stroller. The supply of flags was endless because the developers had planned on building hundreds of homes out there. The surveyors must've spent months placing those flags. Some nights we'd have so many tied to the stroller, we'd look like a big Chinese dragon, flapping down the street.

I'd push Martin up one big hill, and we'd gaze at the sunset behind the city. Some nights, pinks and oranges smudged and flared all over the sky, but other nights the sky was clogged with the filthy grays and browns that the L.A. transplants had dragged to our desert.

. . .

ANN WAS THE first person I met when I moved to Tucson from Manhattan, and she didn't really let me meet anyone else. She certainly didn't have a vast circle of friends. She happened to be the associate at the bank who set up my checking and savings accounts the second day I was in town, and she called me that night, saying, "I know you're new here, and I thought you could use a home-cooked meal." She gave me the whole business, and the more I learned about her—she hated her job, couldn't afford to go back to college, mother died when she was ten, apartment complex smelled like pesticide, car in a constant state of disrepair— the more I got sucked in.

It wasn't just pity. She was different then, enthusiastically showing me Tucson, like she had been waiting her whole life for someone new to show it to. "Just wait until August when the monsoons come and lightning lights the sky. . . . They whitewash the big A every year for U of A's homecoming. . . . The Pima County Fair . . . blah, blah, blah . . ."

We hiked in the Santa Catalinas, drove down to Nogales and bought blankets and got drunk on tequila, looked through the telescopes at the planetarium, went to all the museums, ate at all the little Mexican places on South Sixth Avenue. She was still showing me the city when we got married, still planning weekend outings after Martin was born. I think we finally exhausted the city a few weeks after we moved into the model home.

I STAYED UP and waited for Ann and Clarissa each time they went out. Wednesday nights nothing was on TV, especially out there, where we couldn't get cable, so I'd do the housework that Clarissa had neglected all week and try to forget the envy and hostility churning in my stomach.

One of those Wednesday nights, I was folding laundry when the two of them returned home. I had it neatly stacked up on the couch to make them feel guilty. They were ruddy from laughing as they walked in.

"Where'd you guys go tonight?" I asked them. I refolded a pair of black panties that had been on the top of the stack. Clarissa and Ann stopped laughing.

"We're not *guys*," Clarissa said, and she snatched the panties out of my hands like I had been sniffing them or something.

"Is Martin asleep?" Ann asked.

"Yes," I said.

That's how most nights were. I pictured them out on the town, stuffing dollar bills in the G-string of some greased-up, rippled male stripper, or line-dancing with cubicle cowboys at the Cactus Moon Cantina.

Another night, before the two of them went out, Ann and I were sitting on the couch in front of the TV, only the TV wasn't on. I had my arm around her, was kissing her ear, hiding under her hair, making her smile. We had talked about her job, how she was beginning to like it better since her boss got transferred. It was the best ten minutes I had spent alone with her that entire summer. Then Clarissa popped in from the kitchen and ruined it.

"Do you want to go back to BHT tonight?" she asked Ann—loudly, rudely.

"I don't know if I can handle two nights in a row," Ann said. She stood up and conspiratorially ushered Clarissa back toward the kitchen.

"You-know-who might be there," Clarissa said. "And those boots!"

They laughed and disappeared into the kitchen, leaving me in front of the blank TV, wondering.

. . .

THE BENCHES WERE breaking that summer. We made them where I worked. I went to four years of college and two years of architecture school to draw cement benches. The design offices were attached to the plant, so everything in my work area stank of cement dust. At the end of each day, my teeth were gritty and my hair was like a powdered wig.

In the center of each bench, there was a stress point that hadn't been accounted for by Quality Control. We'd get calls from customers whose benches had broken, and Lou, the manager, would hook his dimpled fingers over the top of my cubicle, peer at me, and say, "Another one of your benches broke, guy," like it was all my fault. It wasn't. If they had used the cement mix I had suggested when I originally designed the benches, instead of the cheapo aerated mix, there wouldn't have been any problems.

For all of June, I had pretended to be hard at work designing a cement trash can. I could have done it in three days if I had really tried, but it was difficult to get enthusiastic about a trash can—especially a cement one—so I wrote fake memos to the material scientists, flipped through OSHA manuals, played Tetris on my computer.

The only person I liked in the whole company was Lou's secretary, Franny, a trendy woman who behaved like an eighth grader. Every other weekend she drove seven hours to the outlet stores near Palm Springs. It was an Armani summer for her, a summer of muted linen pants and clunky, industrial-looking black boots.

"These shoes would have cost me three hundred dollars in L.A., and I got them for ninety," she said, pointing her toe, rolling her leg from side to side.

"Good deal," I said. "Just don't kick me."

She'd cut me through and let me listen when Lou made his calls for male escorts on Friday afternoons. Lou's first question to the call boy was always "Do you do fats?" Then it was "What do you look like? Buff?" And we'd hear the poor guy list his stats, trying to sell himself to blubber-ass Lou.

On the week of the Fourth of July, Lou was gone for an extra three days, which meant Franny could snoop around in his office.

"Ed, I found something juicy," she told me that Wednesday after lunch. "Right there in the bottom drawer, under a bunch of old inventory folders, behind the first-aid kit." Her hands were trembling, she was dancing.

She had discovered a leather-bound scrapbook filled with clippings of Scott Baio. They were mostly from old *Tiger Beat* or *Teen Dream* magazines, back when Scott was on TV all the time as Chachi in *Happy Days,* or Charles in *Charles in Charge.* Toward the end of the book was a meticulously handwritten log of all the different episodes, plus the other times Lou had seen Scott Baio, like on *Circus of the Stars* or as Johnny Carson's guest. There were a few *TV Guide* ads for the more recent shows Scott had been doing, but these were just paper-clipped in a clump to the last page, like Lou hadn't had time to start a second volume. The book was alive: Orderly Obsession, Absolute Devotion, True Love! I imagined faithful Lou combing the magazines in Safeway, watching videotaped episodes of *Happy Days,* writing letters to Scott. Maybe it was somewhat reciprocal, maybe Scott's publicist had sent him form letters and glossy photos showing Scott in a different pose each year. Whatever the case, Lou had it bad: he had the Love Drive.

"I'm leaving," I told Franny. I closed the book and wiped

my hands on my pants. It was only two in the afternoon, but I was anxious, taken aback by this discovery. Plus, I just wanted to leave, and Lou wasn't there to tell me I couldn't.

"You can't," she said. She grabbed my wrist and stroked the hair on my arm with her thumb. "I might find something better."

"You might, but I really gotta go."

"Party pooper," she said, defeated. She picked up the scrapbook, shoved it back in the bottom drawer, and kicked the drawer shut with her meaty boot.

I started on my way home, past the airport expressway and past the dusty fairgrounds, before I decided to turn around and away. Clarissa would have just been slouched on the couch watching *Oprah* anyway. I would have walked in and asked her if she had done anything all day, and she would have told me to get a life of my own—and she would have been sort of right.

The Bay Horse Tavern was where I first stopped. Maybe it was the bold orange sign with the stupid-looking, googly-eyed cartoon stallion that snagged me. Maybe it was because the Bay Horse was right next to Dime Vid, a place where you could play outdated video games for a dime. Ann never let me play video games at home. She never let me drink beer, either. "You want to get fat?" she'd say. "Beer makes men fat. Fat men have breasts."

I ordered a dollar bottle of Bud and looked at the Polaroids of the regulars pinned up behind the bar. In each of the pictures, the people pressed their faces together cheek-to-cheek, smiled, and held up whatever they were drinking. When I saw the one of Ann and Clarissa, I gulped my beer and changed stools so I could get a better look. Both of their faces were flashed white, their eyes red as devils, but it was definitely them. A third woman, whose face was also somewhat washed away, was squished between them, and a mustachioed man in a satin Wildcats jacket looked as if he had popped himself in the camera's view at the last second. All smiles, all holding beers.

"See that picture there," I said to the bartender, pointing with my beer bottle.

She was bending over at the other end of the bar, wiping down the inside of a refrigerator. She sighed and trudged across the rubber mats behind the bar, her soiled tennis shoes making squeaking, rubber-on-rubber noises. "Which?" she said.

"That one," I said, standing, pointing with my bottle.

"Ann, Jenny, Clarissa, and that guy from the dart tournament," she said matter-of-factly, like I had challenged her to name them all. She flipped her feathered red hair over her shoulder.

"Clarissa's only eighteen," I said. "Shouldn't be allowed in here. Can I have another?" I held up my bottle.

She popped open another beer for me and said, "How do you know?"

"She's my niece, and Ann's my wife."

The bartender's lip curled up on one side, and she spit out a laugh. "You're Ed," she said. "I've heard about you."

"Oh?"

"Yes." She resumed her cleaning of the fridge.

I ordered three more beers and pounded them, still looking at the photos of the regulars. "Tell Ann and Clarissa I said hello when they come in tonight," I said to the bartender as I was leaving, pushing the door into the white burst of sun.

"They only come on Tuesdays and Thursdays," she said.

. . .

I WAS BUZZED and bloated as I waddled over to Dime Vid in the blazing afternoon heat.

The woman working at Dime Vid smiled broadly at me when I walked in. I was the only one in there besides her. She was old, maybe seventy, but she wore bright, plastic little-girl barrettes in her long gray hair. "You've just been drinking next door," she said.

"Yes," I said. I handed her a buck. "Dimes, please."

She counted me the dimes from her change belt and disappeared. I put three in Asteroids.

I didn't do very well at Asteroids. In my first game, I lost all three ships before she returned with two beers. My score was around 2,000. You need 10,000 for a free ship.

She handed me an icy Coors, already popped open. If I had known the Dime Vid lady was giving out free beers, I would have gone there first and skipped the Bay Horse. "Thanks," I said.

"You're playing all wrong," she said. "Save one asteroid on the screen, and wait for the flying saucers to come out."

She swigged her beer and shifted her dentures with a clicking sound. Her electric-pink gums and her white teeth were too perfect. They looked wrong in the middle of her weathered, roasted face. "Let me guess," she said. "You're a doctor and you came to relieve some stress."

"I design cement benches," I said. "Now I design cement trash cans." I ran my fingers through my hair to show her the cement dust. She didn't notice.

"Out early for the holiday weekend?"

"A book of Scott Baio pictures scared me." I took my last swig of beer. It was still cold enough to hurt my teeth. I lost my second ship then. It exploded with a dry poof at around 8,000.

"Chachi?"

I tried to explain Lou's Love Drive, how it frightened me a little, and I forgot about the strategy that she had suggested. I blithely blasted away at all the floating asteroids on the screen. Only one saucer came out. I missed it.

"You know," she said, "you can love all different people and things, but when you dig through it all—save that last asteroid—when you dig through it all, the love is the same."

"Only sometimes it's illegal," I said.

IT WAS A LITTLE tough behind the wheel for me. I made it to the Taco Bell drive-through window all right, ate three burritos in the parking lot with the engine running and the air-conditioning on full blast. From there I drove a few blocks to the liquor store to buy a six-pack. As I pulled into the parking lot, I scraped the side of my car on a bus-stop sign. The noise it made, that high-pitched grinding squeal, was funny at the time. I lost my side mirror. I was going to get beer, and bring it home, and drink it there, and maybe get fat and grow big-ass tits—all in front of Ann.

I decided that I was bound for jail if I got pulled over, so I cracked open a beer in the car and held it between my thighs.

Ann had probably been home from work for a few hours, I imagined, and she and Clarissa would have to keep sitting around, waiting for me, before they could go out.

I drove east, away from the eye-level sun, to the dead planes near the Air Museum. I skidded into the dirt next to a tall chain-link fence topped with evil twists of prison-quality barbed wire. Every fifty feet or so along the fence, there was a red sign: ABSOLUTELY NO TRESPASSING. GUARD DOGS ON DUTY. PROPERTY OF THE U.S. ARMED FORCES. Bullshit, I thought, looking at all the junked planes. Where would the dogs be? They'd die in the heat. I wanted in the Boneyard. I wanted to climb around on a Convair B-58—not that I remembered exactly what one looked like. I wanted to sit in the cockpit and drink my five and a half beers.

I didn't do it.

That sharp, flesh-ripping barbed wire scared me—so did the nonexistent dogs—and I chickened out. Still, I had my beer, and I cracked another as I headed home.

THEY WERE ALL primped and ready to leave when I walked in. Ann was wearing way too much makeup, and her hair was sprayed tall in the front like a bug shield. Clarissa had the same hair going. Proudly, I held the four remaining beers in front of me.

"You're late," Ann said. "And drunk?"

"These are my beers," I said. "And I'm your fat, beer-drinking husband."

"Ed, you're not fat," Ann said. Her eyebrows looked thin. Plucked away.

"I wanna be," I said.

"No beer," she said. "What's with you?"

I walked up to them, and Clarissa retreated to the kitchen. I looked at Ann's eyes: lined in black. They told me she wasn't happy to see me. She hadn't been nervously waiting for me to get home, calling the office, checking up on me. She wasn't relieved that I hadn't died in a car wreck.

I realized then that I wouldn't have kept a scrapbook of Ann pictures. I wouldn't have logged all of her appearances if she had been on TV. I wouldn't have spent that much time thinking about her, and I never would. I staggered to the bathroom.

I was thinking, as I stood there in front of the toilet, that

I should be back in the Convair B-58 Hustler, casually finishing my beer, fiddling with the busted controls, staring up at the swarm of stars beginning to shine in the sky. But I was a wuss, so instead I was back at home, taking a piss, watching the bowl bubble up.

"Where's Martin?" I asked when I returned to the family room.

"Asleep," Ann said. "Clarissa and I are going out now. Are you okay here?" She gathered her purse and keys from the couch, not waiting for me to answer. "Get rid of that beer."

"Have fun," I said. Then I pushed open the kitchen door and also told Clarissa to have fun. She responded by telling me that a girl in her high school was killed by a drunk driver, and then she sneered at me more dramatically than she ever had, lifting her lip and arching her painted-on brows.

"Your hair looks really pretty," I told her.

MARTIN DIDN'T WAKE UP when I strapped him in his stroller. I brought a beer on our walk. I had put the other three in the refrigerator, shoving Ann's yogurt way in the back, next to the gallon jug of generic barbecue sauce we never used. It was dark outside, and I knew that this would have to be a short walk.

I pushed Martin around our cul-de-sac. The Mormons didn't have any lights on. I imagined they were probably asleep, the girls in beds lined up like in a hospital ward, wearing long, flannel nightgowns and sleeping caps pulled down over their scrubbed foreheads.

The Romboughs' home was lit up. Through the big window, I could see them sitting around the dining-room table, wearing party hats. There was a cake, and shiny Mylar balloons were everywhere. One of the balloons had a purple 8 on it. It was Romboner's birthday. Romboner was clapping and smiling and shrieking. They were fussing over him good: adjusting his bib, kissing him on his crinkly monkey lips, singing to him. I bet they had a great scrapbook of Romboner. From the start, they must have taken lots of photos of him.

Martin stirred in his stroller and yawned. He sleepily pointed to the Romboughs and said, "Nan."

"No," I said. "Those are the Romboughs." I pushed the stroller up their driveway with one hand while I drank the last bit of beer. I tossed the can into an oleander and held Martin up so he could press their glowing doorbell.

Lady Rombough opened the door. The dentist and the chimp were looking on from their places at the birthday table. "May I help you, Ed?"

"No," I said, and I put Martin back in his stroller. The chimp showed me his big teeth—not in the threatening I-want-to-monkey-fuck-your-wife way, but in a playful way.

"What do you need?" she asked.

I looked back at the dentist and Romboner. "Honestly," I said, "I'm not too sure."

love them

FOR YEARS, SNIDER had watched his mother, Elena, feature herself as *all that.* So tonight, when Elena peeked her rain-wet head into the kitchen, made kissy noises, and alerted Snider and his two buddies Ham and Phon-Tip to a frog orgy in the swimming pool, Snider was not at all surprised. The three boys put down their beers and poker hands and followed her outside to check it out.

"They aren't frogs," Snider said, pointing. "They're Colorado River toads."

"I don't give a shit what they are," Ham said, standing on the diving board, scratching his belly.

"Hey!" Elena said. "You kiss your mother with that dirty mouth?" She flicked her tongue like a rock star.

Snider was disgusted and sighed loudly to let his mother know. Ham and Phon-Tip sniggered.

"Sorry," Elena said in her sexiest contralto. She bent over and squeezed rain from the hem of her dress. "Inappropriate tongue gesture."

Everyone stood on the deck and watched in the electric-purple light as a fat female kicked through the deep end with a peewee male clinging to her back. Strings of her black, jellied eggs trailed and hung in the water. Unhitched toads, about a dozen, swam around as well, producing quiet ripples. A few others croaked from the tall grass by the filter pumps.

Snider reached over the stucco wall and grabbed the net.

"Leave them alone!" Elena said. "Let them love!" She walked over to Phon-Tip, her muscular, full hips preceding her in every step. She began to massage his shoulders and purr. Her light dress and skimpy undergarments were saturated, clinging, revealing the details of her body to the boys, even in the thin light radiating from the pool.

"Chlorine will kill them," Snider said.

Elena used a goo-goo voice and rested her chin on Phon-Tip's shoulder: "Tippy, tell my son to leave those frogs alone." She ran her fingers through Phon-Tip's fresh flattop.

"He's right about the chlorine," Phon-Tip said. He stepped away from Elena and patted his hair. "And don't call me Tippy, please."

Snider scooped the mating toads in the net. He felt their weight in his wrists and flung them over the wall. They were still love-linked as they crashed into a copse of kumquat bushes.

"Coitus interruptus," Ham said.

"I don't like you boys anymore," Elena said.

"Snider was the one who did it," Ham said. "Not me."

"I saw your father last night," Elena said to Snider, almost vindictively. "He was at the Bashful Bandit handing out Jesus pamphlets."

"That's a nice place for you to be," Snider said, snagging another toad in the net. The Bashful Bandit was a motorcycle bar on the edge of Tucson's scanty red-light district. It scared him to think that his mother was socializing with Hell's Angels, junk-sick hookers, and the other lowlifes he imagined might go there. He pitched the toad into the dark desert.

"I have a life," Elena said. "Besides, the Wise One was there at the same bar."

"He was distributing pamphlets," Snider said. "Who knows what you were doing there."

"Who knows," Elena said. She did a little twirl, head cocked toward the newly exposed stars. "You have any beer left?" She collapsed onto a rain-beaded chaise and kicked off her sandals.

All three boys lied without hesitation: "No."

Ham and Phon-Tip had never called Elena "Mrs. Snider." She was nothing like a Mrs., and legally she was no longer a Mrs., anyway. Snider's father had long ago abandoned his wife and son for religion and confused, wayward girls. He preached halfway across the city at the Y-Our Church of THE WORD where his parishioners dubbed him "the Wise One." Snider often saw his father's '73 Chevrolet El Camino parked in the brown lawn of the cinder-block church, next to the sign that read NO JESUS, KNOW FEAR. KNOW JESUS, NO FEAR. The Wise One had meticulously painted the Stations of the Cross on the car-truck, with the final phase of crucifixion rendered in full but sun-faded color on the hood. Like most people in Tucson, Snider found his father's automobile creepy. Up close, Jesus too closely resembled Cher.

The Wise One, back when he was known as Kenny, brought Elena to the States from Honduras. Kenny had served in the Peace Corps teaching fish farming to the locals outside Tegucigalpa. One sultry night, a few months before the end of his two-year tour, Elena cornered him at El Bar Super Puerco, where she had been making the rounds with her girlfriends, hoping to snare a gringo. She spotted him before anyone else—his innocent eyes—and after she took him upstairs to a thickly humid stall and treated him to a few things that a twenty-four-year-old, peace-loving biology major from Vanderbilt had never experienced, he asked if he could see her again. She was pregnant with Snider by the time Kenny's assignment ended.

Elena spent her first three years in America locked in front of sitcoms and soap operas, repeating the actors' lines, dropping her Honduran accent, filling the gaps in her English. "I'd sit there and say things like 'Sit on it, Potsie' or 'Andy, you're an alcoholic and we need to talk' over and over. Kenny thought I was loco, but I thought he was, so I figured, what the hell. . . ."

Snider was weirdly proud of Elena the first time he had secretly listened to her tell this story to a friend on the telephone. He liked how she portrayed herself as the tricky one, his father, Kenny, the duped.

SNIDER HAD THE most tolerable summer job of the boys. He was the Bicycle Burrito Boy at Nico's Taqueria in downtown Tucson. Paid to deliver spicy meals in Styrofoam packages to grumpy, wan cubicle workers. It was frequently over one hundred degrees, but he enjoyed riding his bicycle, his tires humming along the streets. The heat pumping up from the asphalt made him feel alive, like a survivor, and his ruddy and sweat-glazed face elicited good tips. Plus Snider got to work with Cissy, a Gamma Phi Beta at the University of Arizona who had perfectly pointed eyebrows and an aerobicized body. She wasn't snobby, and even though she knew Snider was three years her junior, she flirted with him and commented on his nice ass. She packed the lunches for delivery at Nico's Taqueria; she and Snider were a team. Each weekday at ten-thirty, when Snider punched in, she'd be positioned at the counter in the back, stuffing small paper bags with tortilla chips, swaying her khaki shorts to the Top 40 music from the radio.

Today when Snider arrived, Cissy was sweating over a messy pot of refried beans gurgling on the stove. "Paco's sick," she told Snider, stirring the heavy goop with a wooden spoon. "We gotta do all his shit." Her face was steamed. Droplets of condensation had gathered on her fragile jawline. The sun pushing through the blurred windows made her glow, lit her hair into fresh hues of red and mahogany Snider had never noticed.

"Bummer." Snider sat on the counter next to the big stove and stuck his finger in the warm beans. He tasted them. They needed salt. "So, when are you taking me barhopping?"

She ignored him or didn't hear him, lifting the spoon, letting some beans plop back into the pot. "I hate these." She reached over and turned the burner to low. "You'll be on your bike nonstop today. We already have, like, twenty orders."

"Barhopping?" Snider said. "You promised."

Wiping her wet forehead with a paper towel, she whooped and smiled. "Hot." Then she wadded the paper towel and threw it at Snider. "Tuesday after work we'll go to the Green Dolphin, and then over to Dirtbags."

As Cissy had warned, Snider had no rest from his bike that

day, but he cleared thirty-one dollars in tips, and as he was pedaling home into the white afternoon sun, swigging tepid Gatorade from his squeeze bottle, he thought, This is all easy. He had about two hours at home before Ham and Phon-Tip showed up. He might flop around in the pool or lounge on the couch and click back and forth between talk shows.

But Elena was home early from the bank where she worked as a teller. Her sedan was parked in the gravel driveway next to a raised, gloss-black Chevy four-by-four with monster tires and flashy magnesium rims. Snider felt like turning around when he saw the unfamiliar truck. He briefly considered leaving a note on the gate for Ham and Phon-Tip, telling them to meet him at the rec center, but sweat was coursing down his neck and back, he stank, and he knew he should go inside and make sure his mother wasn't in any trouble.

Snider shoved the gate open and saw a skinny man sitting on the edge of the pool. The guy's shoulder blades protruded sharply, casting black triangles over his zitty back. As Snider wheeled his bike closer, he read the blue tattoo that spanned the man's atrophied bicep: BAD BOY.

The man turned, lifting his legs out of the pool, and stood. The fly of his cutoffs was down. He squinted at Snider. "Elena's inside with Russ," he said. "Who are you?"

Snider ignored the guy's question. He propped his bike against the picnic table and unbuckled his butt-pack. "Your barn door's open, and your chicken's trying to get out," Snider told him, pointing at his fly. Snider didn't want to go into the house and see this Russ. He knew from this guy's military hair that Elena had been trolling for men down in Sierra Vista, near Fort Huachuca.

. . .

SNIDER WAS TOO familiar with Elena's cruising. As a kid, he'd spent many hours in the Captain Buffet, a chicken-fried steak place a few miles from the fort. Elena had claimed that the best men were big eaters who weren't fat. "They're peppy," she said, snapping her fingers like a belly dancer. Mother and son watched each man as he approached the buffet. If they spotted a lean one heaping food onto his tray, Elena would prance over and start her coquettish routine. She'd drop a utensil, and if the man didn't pick it up for her, she'd bend over to get it herself and aim her pear-shaped ass at him. Snider had witnessed the method often, and each time he'd pray it wouldn't work so he wouldn't have to wait in the car.

Sometimes she'd had to settle for civilians, even overweight or geriatric ones, but her stints at the Captain Buffet always paid off. Snider would sit in the car, coloring or reading comic books, while Elena was off loving the men. She had told young Snider that God made women to be with men, and since his father left, she had to find new men. "It's like praying," she told him. "God wants me to. God wants me to love these men." He bought it for a while, he'd seen the pictures of Adam and Eve in his children's Bible, he'd remembered hearing from his father that he was supposed to love everyone, even his enemies. *God is love.*

He hated the wait. Even though he believed his mother was doing good, he was scared for her. She'd park her car outside each man's place: a trailer, a decaying apartment complex, or the sad, drab government prefab homes that clogged the town. Often Snider waited for over an hour in the hot car, attempting to stay in the lines of the Captain Buffet coloring book with melting crayons that clumped and smeared over the pages. He'd peek at the stick-on digital clock on the dash and try not to think about what the man might be doing to his mother. At twenty minutes the man was tying her up. At thirty he was strangling or stabbing her. At forty he was burying her. And at fifty he was on his way to get Snider. Snider always locked the doors and rolled up the windows, making it even hotter in the car.

Snider was nine when he asked Elena if she was fucking the men. "Do you know what that means?" she asked. "Duh," he said, and he repeatedly rammed a purple Crayola into the crayon sharpener built into the box. She left Snider at home from that day on, warning him to stay out of the pool and to keep the doors bolted.

INSIDE THE HOUSE, Elena and this Russ, a husky guy with a broad, sunburned nose, were stretched on the couch, Elena's hand up his T-shirt. The TV was tuned to a loud baseball game. Snider stood in the doorway and rolled his eyes in disgust.

"What?" Elena said to Snider.

"What do you think?"

Elena separated herself from Russ, smoothed her skirt, and walked over to her son.

Snider could detect a glandular odor on her, something musky—a sex smell, he figured. It was just like her to sell herself short, to end up with someone like the man sprawled on the couch.

"I don't have to answer to you," she whispered. "I never will."

"Just get him out of here before Ham and Phon-Tip show up." Snider headed down the hall toward his bedroom and added, "Get rid of the dork by the pool, too."

. . .

FOR MOST OF Snider's junior high years, Elena had quit picking up soldiers and became a regular at the Fine Line, a dance club for the sexually ambiguous. Even though she didn't leave the house until ten or eleven at night, Snider felt she was safe out partying with drag queens and gay men— safer than sleeping with desperate strangers down by the fort. She'd be home from the Fine Line by seven A.M., stinky with cigarettes and rotting perfume, in time to wake Snider for school and send him off. That nudge from her in the morning was comforting. She was home. She was happy. And she hadn't been down to Fort Huachuca or the Captain Buffet. Over breakfast she'd relate the events of the previous night to curious Snider, starting first with the queens' outfits and hairstyles, and then onto mishaps, snubbings, and bitchy backstabbings. Snider was one of the few seventh graders in Tucson who knew the difference between transsexuals and transvestites. He knew that mules were lounge wear, not evening wear, knew the names of ephemeral clubs in New York and Los Angeles.

Each afternoon when Snider returned home from school, Elena's friends from the Fine Line would be gathered around the TV in the family room, watching *Days of Our Lives* or *As the World Turns:* "When in the hell is Marlena gonna stop trying to work that same tired Farrah hair? . . . If I wrote for this show, Holden would be having an affair with Damian. . . ." As Snider walked in, they'd turn down the soap operas, and Yummi—sporting one of her swirled, psychedelic housedresses—would heat up some canned spaghetti or a tamale and serve Snider the snack on a metal tray. They'd all hear about his day at school and ask him questions about his friends and teachers, whom they knew by name.

Yummi faithfully attended Snider's soccer games, often

accompanied by two or three other queens. Fully decked, they'd rabidly cheer. They wouldn't sit near Elena, and they made sure not to root for Snider specifically. He'd hear the *clomp-klunk, clomp-klunk, clomp-klunk* of their platforms on the metal bleachers, and when he'd glance up there from his position on the field, he'd see their big, brilliant hair and hear them screaming like they genuinely cared if his team won.

Yummi helped Snider on Halloween, meticulously painting his face until he looked dead, like a real zombie. It was Snider's job to pop up from behind a cardboard grave and scare visitors to the eighth-grade Haunted Gymnasium. The tiny paintbrushes were cold, and they tickled as Yummi dabbed theater makeup onto his face. Every once in a while, her whiskery wrist would graze Snider's cheek, and he'd be reminded that she was really a he.

"You go through this every day?" Snider asked.

"Go through what, hon?" Yummi said, tracing Snider's eye in gray shadow.

"The makeup."

"Been doing it for years." She fluttered her exaggerated false eyelashes. Each lash had a tiny colored ball on its tip— like miniature Easter eggs. "I started at Halloween when I was about your age."

Snider was dejected when his mother quit going to the Fine Line and Yummi and the girls stopped coming by. He dreaded coming home after school to no one, to an empty, silent house. He'd click on the TV and watch bad reruns until his dull headache set in and signaled it was time for a bowl of cereal. He missed his mother, Yummi, and the others. He had liked having a captive audience each afternoon, and he had liked knowing his mother had real friends, friends who had visited more than once or twice.

"I can't keep up with them," Elena finally explained to Snider one evening over Chinese takeout. "They do more than dress up and go dancing, you know—bad things."

"You could still be friends with them," Snider said. "You could let them watch TV here."

"I've been cleaned from their cupboard," she said blankly. She bit into an egg roll and spit something pink onto her paper plate. "I'm like a dusty can of cocktail wieners."

"What?"

"They tossed me."

"There was a message on the machine from Yummi yesterday."

"She wanted her palazzo pants back," Elena said. "Not that she can squeeze them over all that cellulite."

"She's not that fat."

"Besides," Elena said, "drag queens are over. Everyone's sick of them."

Snider had never seen Yummi out of drag—as a man—until a few weeks after Elena's expulsion from the group. He looked through Yummi's sliding-glass door one morning, about to knock and intending to patch things up between her and his mother, when he saw her: wigless, with a bleached crewcut and day-old, smudged makeup, sitting at her kitchen table with a friend. It was the friend who frightened Snider. He was older. The wrinkles that sprouted from his eyes were deep, and his jowls sagged. But he was dressed like a boy, like Snider: Air Jordans (untied), baggy surfer shorts, a White Sox T-shirt, and a ball cap turned backward. A new skateboard was propped against his chair, the wheels still beaming Popsicle red. Yummi was feeding the man cereal like the man was a baby, brushing the spoon on his chin to catch stray drops of milk before they squirmed down. Snider never did knock, but Yummi's friend noticed him. The man jumped up like he was about to kick Snider's ass for intruding.

Snider ran, chugging down Fourth Avenue, past thrift stores and street people, until he made it to the spray-painted underpass, where he slowed in the flyblown shadows. He had heard Yummi yelling after him the whole way—"What did you want, sugar? Tell your mama she knows my number when she's ready to apologize!"—but he didn't turn around.

ON HIS WAY home from work on Tuesday, the planned bar-hopping day, Snider ran over something, and his front tire hissed wickedly until it was flat, thumping on the pavement. When he pulled onto the dirt shoulder of Grande Avenue and reached for his fanny pack, he realized he had left it at work, on the shelf above the cluttered desk. Not only were his extra bike tube and tools in the pack, but his wallet with his fake ID and the day's tips were in there as well. He didn't even have a quarter to call Nico's Taqueria. He pushed his bike back toward downtown. Two miles in the killer sun, unreachable silver mirages sizzling up from the streets.

After he retrieved his pack and fixed the flat, he realized he'd have to haul ass to get home in time to meet Cissy, who was picking him up early for ten-cent beers at the Green Dolphin. He had planned on killing a twelve-pack with Ham and Phon-Tip before she got there, but now there was no time. His thighs burned, and salty sweat stung his eyes as he pedaled up the hill in front of the community college.

Russ's polished truck hogged the driveway again. Worse, Cissy's Trooper was parked out front. She was early.

Snider dropped his bike into the pinkish gravel by the front door. He imagined Cissy inside the house, seated between

Elena and Russ on the couch, listening to Elena babble about crazy Kenny and how he screwed her out of a life.

Elena smiled and waved a spatula at Snider when he peeked into his bedroom, then she continued to chat it up with Phon-Tip and Ham, who sat on the floor with comic books and Coors: "I'm about to spark the grill, boys." She wore a tight lavender halter that splayed her breasts. She modeled it, slowly twisting her torso so she could speak over her shoulder. "You better get cleaned up fast," she said to Snider. "Your girlfriend's in the family room playing Nintendo with Russ. She's cute."

"She's not my girlfriend," he said.

"She is cute," Elena said. "Barbecue?"

"No," Snider said. "Can you leave us alone for a second?"

"I wanted you to officially meet Russ," Elena said. "He brought enough ribs for all of us." Elena then smiled at Phon-Tip. "Like I said, Tippy, plenty of beer, too."

Elena called Russ to turn off the game and come greet Snider. Cissy yelled hello from the family room, but Snider was out the front door, into the dense heat again, before Cissy or Russ saw him.

Elena yelled after Snider, and he heard her sandals ripping through the gravel right behind him as he pushed his bike toward the street. He didn't turn around until she grabbed his sunburned shoulder. The urge to shove or punch her was overwhelming, frightening, but he was able to suck in a breath and say, "No."

"Don't you judge me!" Elena yelled, throwing the spatula to the ground. "I got enough of that shit from the Wise One!" Then her words dissolved into a mumbling of Spanish—this hadn't happened in years.

· · ·

EVEN AS A LITTLE KID sitting stiffly in the itchy upholstered pews of the Church of THE WORD, Snider had sensed his father was odd. Before Kenny was even ordained, the parish asked him to recite verses from his dog-eared, floppy Bible. And Kenny'd yell. Flecks of spittle flew from his mouth as he passionately shouted lines in his aristocratic southern drawl. Sometimes Snider would daydream, but certain verses resonated and scared him: *And unclean spirits went out, and entered into the swine; and the herd ran violently down a steep place into the sea, and were choked . . .* He imagined the devil-pigs, red, with bloody fangs, chewing and trampling each other as they charged to their deaths in the black ocean.

The church members turned to Kenny for advice, questioned him about biblical passages, asked him to lead prayer sessions. They often met at Snider's house. Kenny sat in front of the muted, flickering TV for hours before each meeting, scrawling madly into a leather-bound notebook that Snider was never allowed to touch. Snider was in charge of setting up the metal chairs in a circle in the family room, sometimes as many as twelve. Elena prepared snacks—fried plantains or other Honduran delicacies the group wouldn't touch. She never joined in prayer.

When the people arrived, Kenny sprang up and greeted them: always a deep, lingering hug for each. Most of them were women—lost young women who looked sad to Snider.

After the meetings, a few of the women would wander into the rock garden on the side of the house to pray some more. Out his window, Snider could see them in the soft, wavy glow of votive candles, kneeling in the dirt, looking to the night sky with their wild, joke-shop eyes.

It was in that little garden where Snider's father told him that he was becoming a minister and moving to the church. "You'll see me every Sunday when your mother brings you to services," he said. Kenny was digging a hole for a dwarf lime tree. "The parish needs me." His sleeves were rolled up, and a V of sweat soaked through his shirt under his neck.

Snider looked around the garden at the brightly painted wooden crosses adorned with plastic flowers and snapshots of babies and soldiers. He examined the spent votives, some cracked with wax seeping out: Saint Jude, Guadalupe, El Muerte. . . . He wished the women would leave them in someone else's yard. "Who's going to take care of this garden?" he asked his father.

"You," his father said.

"No way."

"You know what the word is on this?" Kenny said. "Children obey your parents in the Lord, for this is right."

"But I hate this garden."

And a few weeks later, the new lime tree was brown and dry—pointy, naked branches like scribbles in the sun against the white stucco wall.

NOW, AFTER TEN YEARS, Snider tried to dismiss his father as just another wacko lurking around Tucson. The last time the Wise One had called him was in May. He had asked Snider to attend a teen testimonial retreat at Young Bible Camp on Mount Graham. "Why? So some psycho can fill me with Pepsi and yell at me for jerking off?" Snider said. The Wise One's response stuck: *The eye that mocketh his father, the ravens of the valley shall pick it out, and the young eagles shall eat it.*

Snider pedaled fiercely through the desert on rocky paths behind the community college, catching air and spitting up dust, weaving through towering saguaros and dense bunches of prickly pear cacti. He barely thought about what Elena might be saying to Cissy back home. Instead, he concentrated on the crude trail, hitting the bumps just right so he could experience that roller-coaster feeling in his gut.

A few straggle-haired little girls in sundresses played on the dried lawn of the church, as if it weren't 110 degrees out. One girl pretended to be a robot while the other shouted commands: cartwheel, high kick, hop, back bend. Snider let his bicycle drop on the crispy grass and walked over to his father's car. It looked as if it hadn't been moved in years. The dash was cracked and crumbling, and desiccated weeds tried to grow in the backseat. Snider opened the door, ignoring the weathered depiction of Jesus hefting the cross. He sat behind the wheel, the hot vinyl burning his thighs, and looked at the vaguely familiar gauges and dials. He snapped on the lap-only seat belt, snapped it off, and clicked open the glove compartment: religious pamphlets, maps, and an old snakebite kit.

"This isn't your car," one of the girls said. She leaned into the window so close that Snider could smell her fruity breath and see bits of dried grass in her mussed hair. "It's my dad's." Scabby impetigo crawled from the corners of her mouth down her chin. It looked sore, picked at. Then Snider fixed on her brilliant eyes—ice blue pools—until the other girl, standing farther back, added, "*Our* dad's." Her frayed dress was too short—it looked as if it had been cut with scissors many washes ago.

Snider closed the glove box. "If you move, I can get out."

The girls stepped aside. The one with the short dress walked up to Snider. "He's in Las Vegas helping people," she said. "If he was here, he could get you put in jail."

. . .

SNIDER KILLED the rest of the afternoon in the arcade at Skate Country, playing Mortal Kombat and skee-ball, listening to the crackly records that the deejay spun for the few skaters looping around the rink. He heard songs that Yummi had played ironically and lip-synched in the living room; songs with spongy keyboards, computerized drums, and earnest European vocalists: ". . . Keep feelin' fascination. . . ." Yummi would perform, using an ice-cream scoop or hairbrush as a microphone, as long as Snider watched and kept laughing. These songs also recalled to Snider the endless car rides down to Fort Huachuca, back when he thought his mother's voice on top of the voices streaming from the radio made the songs better. She had bobbed her head as she sped down I-10, belted out the verses with attitude.

As he slowly rode his bicycle home, the sun dipped into a lake of fire between the dark, jagged mountains, leaving a purple and orange smear in its wake. He knew it was corny, but the sunsets never failed to affect him. This one was like a sci-fi paperback cover, an airbrushing of something postapocalyptic visitors to Mars might see while riding bareback on unicorns. Snider's head was heavy, droning with an afternoon's worth of brutal video games and flashing guilt, but riding into God's flaring splendor helped.

Snider found Elena stretched on the couch, basking in the TV's strobing radiance. As he walked into the room, she turned off the TV and sat in the dark for a second. Snider flicked on the light, and she patted the cushion next to her. He joined her, and she brushed his sweaty bangs off his forehead, her lips mashing like she wanted to say something.

"Did you know the Wise One has two little girls?" Snider said.

"I imagine he has about five or six kids," Elena said.

"You think?"

"At least."

Snider couldn't shake the image of the two ratty girls, his half-sisters, playing in front of the church, acting territorial about the Jesus jalopy. Where'd that one get her blue eyes? Did the two of them have the same mother?

"I like Cissy," Elena said. "She's nice. We barbecued without you. Tippy got drunk, and my Russ drove him home."

Snider didn't speak. He envisioned his father on the sparkling Las Vegas strip, duping some poor, disillusioned showgirl with his religious bullshit, spraying tricky quotations from the Bible into her face, scaring her with images of demon-pigs and eye-picking ravens. He imagined the children the girl would bear: dirty faces, mismatched clothes from the Salvation Army.

Finally, he turned to his mother. "Russ's truck's been in our driveway a few times."

"I like him a lot," she said imploringly.

"Good," Snider said. "I'm glad." He meant it, and it almost startled him.

s_go_om_oe_dthing

GREEDY-ASS DEALERS can't find anything good at Value Village Thrift Center because I get first pick of what comes in. Me and three other guys unload the donation truck and sort in the back lot. Nothing good ever makes it on the floor for anyone to buy—nothing. Last month my booty was pretty impressive: 1969 Fred Flintstone figural bank, a box of uncolored-in *Planet of the Apes* coloring books, *Waltons* board game, *CHiPs* Ponch doll—missing a boot.

At first, I felt guilty as I plundered the donations. But I just walked into the process, and in terms of value, I take much less than everyone else. Chicky, he takes clothes and sells them to Buffalo Exchange down by the university. A Hawaiian shirt from the '50s brings him ten bones; a pair of bell-bottoms, five. And he steals in major bulk. Buffalo Exchange buys any vintage or designer garment if it's in good shape and in season, and then they sell it to students for twice as much. Chicky drags at least two big green-trash-bagsful to Buffalo every Saturday. Chicky has a fucked-up dead left arm, so he can't really take anything but clothes. That's all he's allowed to sort at work anyway.

Daniel and Price take furniture. They know all about furniture, and no one else there does, so there's no jealousy, no competition. I'm not sure how much they get for it, but judging by the life they lead—trips to tropical islands where they run around naked together, a Nissan, a big adobe house over on Second Street—I'd guess quite a bit.

The really obvious, high-end, top-dollar shit—jewelry, stereos, TVs, silverware—this goes directly to my boss: Ram Bahadur Rana. No one else even tries for it anymore. The deal here is too good, and we don't want to screw it up.

Ram's from Nepal. When I started, you could see his shoulder blades and count his ribs through his thin T-shirts. Now blubber drapes over his elbows. He has dimples on his knuckles like a big baby. It's the Western diet, he claims. He's from a high caste in Nepal. Told me once his family was the Nepalese equivalent of the Kennedys. So I asked him what he was doing working in a crumbling thrift store in Tucson. He told me to shut up.

His army of Nepalese brownnosers changes every few weeks. When they arrive in Arizona, they call Ram, and he gives them a job until they find something better. They work inside the store, hanging clothes, sweeping the floor, stealing from the registers. Ram encourages them to find other work because he's afraid they might cut into his profits when they learn what's happening out back in terms of pilfering. Ram's a cheap bastard. He lingers near the Dumpster behind the food co-op at five on Tuesdays and Thursdays and takes semirotten organic fruit. He lives in a notoriously dangerous and cockroachy apartment complex next to a bunch of gang-banging vatos, among spray paint and bullets and jumping low-riders, to save thirty bucks a month. Instead of buying curtains, he tapes newspaper in the windows. But you know he has to be rich. Hundreds of dollars' worth of merchandise is loaded from the collection truck directly into the trunk of Ram's '79 Impala each week. The Impala has no backseat and no seat belts, and the muffler is held up with a coat hanger. And Ram wears whatever comes into Value Village in his hog-ass size. Paint-smeared sweatpants. Super Bowl sweatshirt from 1990, the Forty-Niners. Rotten sneakers. He stinks, too. Smells like scrambled eggs.

I could tell on him. I could call the Beacon Foundation, the organization that runs Value Village and gives the money to retards. I'd tell them what's going on, and list specific examples of items Ram has taken.

Chicky and I drink beers on Friday afternoons across the street at Jaime's before all the frat boys crowd in with their girl-friends. Today was a hot Friday—114, with useless monsoon clouds that never broke. The clouds hovered up there in the eastern sky, silver and gray like aluminum, doing nothing. It's days like this when you're back in the lot, unloading the truck and sorting the donations, nose full of thick mothball fumes and puzzle dust, neck gritty and wet, eyes burning with melted sunscreen—it's days like this that help me feel okay about the collection of old toys I have amassed.

And I found something good today: a *Donny and Marie* record trunk, the size of a small suitcase. Cardboard covered in vinyl. Prints of Donny and Marie and their huge Mormon teeth on each side. Donny's hair looks as dorkish as ever, parted in the middle, hanging neatly over his ears. I bought a beer for Chicky to celebrate the find. I'll look up the value of the record trunk when I get home, but I estimate it at somewhere between thirty and fifty. Mine's in good condition—no rips in the vinyl, no dents in the cardboard—so closer to fifty.

The bar here at Jaime's is shined, but still sticky with beer and smoke residue. The windows are tinted so we can see the people outside in the white sun and they can't see us. The same two rich kids from the foothills are panhandling, squatting under the red, yellow, green, and purple mural of sad Guadalupe on the stucco wall of Value Village. I know they're rich by their three-hundred-dollar combat boots. Plus the blue dye in their hair is bright, not dirty enough. They've come to Fourth Avenue every day this summer. They learned early on not to ask me for spare change.

People filter into Jaime's, let the blinding sun gush across the bar. A guy with feathered hair and suede moccasins laced up to his knees chooses a tired Z.Z. Top song on the jukebox: *She's got legs* . . .

Chicky bobs his head to the music. "I shouldn't be having this beer, Grant," he says. "I want to get home early. We just got cable."

"Cable," I say. "Big deal."

"Just saying," Chicky says. "Twenty-three dollars a month including HBO."

"When I lived with my mom, I spliced it from the neighbors' and bought a descrambler box from Ram for thirty bucks. Got all the titty channels." That was the easiest lifestyle. My mother worked all day and made me dinner when she got home. Then I'd head to Carouso's, an Italian restaurant up Fourth Avenue from Value Village. I bused tables there twenty hours a week. I made pretty good money. I slept late. Woke up and pulled the curtains in the family room, clicked on the Spice channel, and watched softcore pornos while I lounged on the couch. The basic law of softcore porn is that they can't show erections. That rules out several camera angles and makes watching it a semifrustrating experience. The rest of the day, I'd blob around the house, eating cereal in front of normal TV until I got that dull buzzing in my head when *Days of Our Lives* came on. Then it was time to get a beer. I did have a girlfriend for a month or so during that period, and my daily schedule changed a bit for the better.

"I don't get any titty channels," Chicky says. "But I got Eve."

"You got Eve," I mumble, thinking about her. Mrs. Robert Chicowski. Ugly, ugly woman. Nose like it got stuck when she pressed it up against a window.

But somehow Chicky and Eve complement each other. After six years together, they still marvel at each other, still hold hands while they watch TV. "You got Eve."

"You need a woman, Grant," Chicky says. His twisted, shrunken arm is resting on the bar, looking like a big yam just dug up. I want to push it off the bar and out of sight, but I never would.

I drink the last bit of my beer. "Too busy."

ON MONDAY WE'RE out there all day unloading, and I don't find anything good. It never ceases to amaze me what people donate: one shoe from a pair, yellowed underpants, used-up votive candles, trophies, half-eaten bags of Christmas candy, matted wigs—all that shit pours out of the truck every day. And puzzles. We're flooded with stupid puzzles. We're supposed to count the pieces. As if we're going to sit down on the burning asphalt and check to see if all 15,000 pieces are there so some old bastard can spend four hundred hours putting together a faded image of Mount Rushmore.

When Ram gets suspicious and agitated, his face flushes

purple, and he starts huffing and sweating more than usual. This happens when there's nothing good on the truck—like today. "Think you can hide it? I'll kick your asses," he says, waddling out to join us in the pressing heat.

"Just don't sit on us," Price says. Price is wearing ball-hugging dungaree shorts today.

"You wish I'd sit on you," Ram says back, making juicy noises with his lips.

"We're not into bestiality," Daniel yells from inside the truck. He's slowly shoving a dresser, and the legs are making a sickening grinding-screeching against the dusty truck floor. "If you think we're stealing your stuff, why don't you haul your fatness up here and have a look at all this useless crap yourself." Daniel is an anabolic musclehead with meaty shoulders as thick as a bull's, so he can say anything. Ram wouldn't fire any of us. He's afraid we'd tell on him.

So Ram disappears back into the store. Later we appease him with two car stereos and a CB radio.

I go home empty-handed.

CHICKY HAS ME over to dinner on Wednesday night. He and Eve wear matching vintage bowling shirts. Eve's has the name BUBBLES embroidered on it; Chicky's has FRED. The two of them are smiling eerily as they lead me into the family room. In there Eve's friend Martha is working a cigarette, sitting on the couch in front of the nightly news. I met Martha at a party earlier this summer. She's a fireman. She told me about a foam rubber factory that burned in South Tucson. All the poison foam gurgled out onto the street and buried two cars like a snowdrift. The fumes were so toxic that kids playing kickball almost a mile downwind vomited blood. I imagine Martha marched right into the fire wearing a big yellow space suit and sprayed out the fire with chemicals.

"Hey, you," Martha says, smiling.

"Hey, Martha," I say. "You shouldn't be smoking."

"I know." She pulls one more time on her cigarette and stubs it into the potted philodendron. "You look tan." Smoke leaks from her nose.

We get through Eve's vegetable lasagna, which is mostly full of chopped carrots. The whole meal Martha's eyeing me, smiling slightly, like she knows something embarrassing about me or is picturing me in some vivid sexual way. And I'm thinking that this might actually happen.

Martha keeps her blond hair short on account of her job. It shows off her proud neck. She holds her head like a woman in a portrait, chin slightly up in that self-assured way. Eats like someone showed her how. Never touches the fork with her teeth, only takes small bites. Eve takes big bites, clanks the fork with her teeth, and chews everything like it's a super-size gumball. Chicky's a slow eater because of his yam arm. Eve should cut up his food for him, but she doesn't. Carrots are hopping off his plate like bugs. I would cut his lasagna for him, but it might embarrass Eve, make her feel bad.

While Chicky and Eve do the dishes later, Martha and I relax on the itchy couch in front of the blank TV.

"I forget what you do," Martha says.

"I work for the Beacon Foundation."

"Wow, you must have the patience of a saint."

"I guess," I say.

"My cousin is developmentally disabled." Martha hunches closer to me. "The Beacon Foundation in Mesa where she lives got her a job at a factory packing boxes full of packing materials." Martha smells of three things: baby powder, smoke, and oregano. This mix is pleasing; reminds me of my parents' house when my dead smoking father was alive. "She loves her job."

"Great," I say, and I'm thinking again that this might happen—if I make it happen. So I lean into her, lips first, and cup my hand under her breast.

"What the hell?" she says, and she nails my nose with her palm—hard. The pain explodes through my head, and I see twinkles and swirls of brown for a few seconds.

"Hey," I say, holding my nose. "Sorry."

"I was beginning to warm up to you," she says, "but you fucked up, buddy." She stands, yells to the kitchen that she's leaving, and stomps out. I notice her boots through the water in my eyes. Cowboy boots, beaten-up cowboy boots. Boots like she uses them like a cowboy would, riding a big horse through the desert, kicking tied-up cows.

Eve and Chicky hustle in. Eve's sporting sudsy yellow rubber gloves that go past her elbows and into the sleeves of her bowling shirt. "What did you do?" Eve says.

"Nothing," I say, plugging my nose. "She just freaked out."

"Stop lying, Grant," Eve says. "Martha will tell me everything, anyway."

It's hard to take Eve seriously, especially when she's animating her words with those rubber gloves. Chicky's not saying anything, just standing behind his wife smirking.

"It was one of those awkward moments," I say. "We went to kiss, and she brushed her breast on my arm. I think she thinks I grabbed her breast. A misunderstanding."

"You're pathetic," Eve says. "You can leave now."

I HAD A GIRLFRIEND once—Heidi. Big girl. Taller than me by three inches. She had an appetite like a lumberjack, but didn't have much money, so she'd come over to my mom's house when I was living there and eat. My mother grew tired of this habit of Heidi's and asked me to tell her to stop cleaning our cupboards. That's how my month of having sex on a regular basis ended.

"She's broke," I said to my mother.

"Let her eat at her own mother's house," she said. "It's bad enough that I'm still feeding you."

"I thought you liked me living here."

"I do," she said, defeated. She looked tired that night, sitting on the couch rubbing her feet, seeming so old. "I just find it strange that she isn't embarrassed, coming in here, going straight to the refrigerator, making herself bologna sandwiches or burritos. Every time I look, more food is gone. Stuff I know you don't eat."

"She was raised in poverty."

"Then you'd think she'd know the value of the food she steals."

"She doesn't steal," I said. "I told her to make herself at home."

"Either you talk to her about it, or I will." She continued rubbing her foot, kneading it like she was working out a splinter. "And when are you going to fix the kitchen window? Or pull up that dead shrub? Or fix the garage door?"

"I need those screws."

"Then get them."

"You should get some different shoes," I said, looking at her old ones on the floor. They were typical nursing shoes: white but scuffed, with the tread worn smooth.

"Too bad I spend all my money on groceries for your girlfriend."

That next day when Heidi came over after work, I clicked off the TV and followed her into the kitchen. She began to prepare herself a salad, picking artichoke hearts out of a jar.

"My mother's pissed," I told her.

"About?" She was chewing on something, focusing on the salad in front of her. "You want some of this?" She pulled the plastic off a head of lettuce and began to rip the lettuce to shreds.

"No, thanks," I said. "I had cereal. Look, I think my mother bought those artichoke hearts for a special recipe or something."

She turned around and faced me. She had probably been to the tanning salon because her face had that damaged orange tint, like the lox she had eaten earlier that week. "I didn't see a note on the jar."

"It's your eating all the food that she's pissed about."

"I don't eat all the food," she said. "Besides, you eat at my apartment all the time."

"I know." I had only ever eaten some chewy crackers and drunk a Coors Light at her apartment.

"Did you tell her that?"

"Sort of."

That didn't do it for Heidi. She stopped making the salad, left all the ingredients there on the counter, grabbed her purse, and went.

Before that day, our routine had been this: Heidi'd fix some food for herself, we'd have a few beers, we'd have sex for an hour or so. Then she'd eat some more, brush her teeth, wash her face, and leave—usually before my mother got home, but not always. I was used to this. My body was used to this. After she left that day, I settled on the couch and tried really hard not to turn on the Spice sex channel.

My mother came home and found me sitting there in that brown afternoon light. "I noticed you still haven't fixed the garage door," she said. She sat on the couch next to me and pulled off her shoes.

"You only reminded me about it yesterday."

"A patient, a big schizophrenic guy your age, he bit me today," she said, rolling up her sleeve to show me. "And after I got my tetanus shot and was putting on this bandage, I was thinking, what is Grant doing right now? And I thought, he's at home watching pornographic movies in his underwear, drinking beer."

"I was not."

"Well, I had another scenario in mind. You and Heidi having sex in my bed, then Heidi making herself a feast and leaving a mess for me to clean." My mother rubbernecked to see into the kitchen. She sighed when she spotted the salad ingredients on the counter. "I hope those aren't my artichoke hearts."

"We never had sex in your bed."

"So later on today, as I was helping a sad Thorazined patient eat pudding—he's younger than you, only twenty-seven—I came to a conclusion that you won't like."

"What?"

"I'm not helping you any by letting you live here." She folded her arms across her chest.

"Yes, you are," I said. "Of course you are. Rent's a lot for just a small apartment."

"I'm not talking about financial help. The sagging garage door is testimony to what I'm talking about. So is that dead saltbush."

"Huh?"

"Think about it. You were in junior high when I was your age."

I moved out at the end of the month. I rented a little adobe bungalow in the middle of town not far from my mother's. Around that time was when I started to work at Value Village. A life change, my mother called it. She said if you don't go through a life change at least every ten years, you stagnate, you rot, your vices dominate.

I called Heidi seventeen times after the day she abandoned the salad ingredients on the counter. I left messages saying I'd take her out to dinner, drive her to the outlet malls in Casa Grande, but she never called back.

DANIEL AND PRICE used to come into Carouso's about twice a week for romantic dinners on the patio. They were good tippers, and they knew the names of the whole wait staff. They insisted on me as their busboy because I gave them free wine and little wicker baskets of bread. Daniel and Price were the ones who told me I should work days at Value Village. I should talk to Ram, they said, and I did.

Ram said to me when I asked him if he had any work, "Are you dumb?"

"No."

"You know a good thing when you see it?"

"Yes."

"You know anything about furniture, vintage clothes, antiques, jewelry, or electronics?"

"Not much," I said. "Fixed an electric fan once. Put on a new plug."

He stared at my eyes. His own eyes were as dark as tar. "We'll try you out back," he said skeptically. "Tomorrow at nine."

I figure he either thought I was too stupid to realize what was going on, or he trusted me as a fellow crook right away. When I found an old *Get Smart* Thermos the first day, and I said I thought it was cool, Ram told me to take it home.

"I can't," I said. "It might be worth something. It's from 1966, and there's not a scratch on it."

"Take it," he said. "Why should some antique dealer get it? They'll just sell it. Take it."

Price walked over and grabbed the Thermos from my hand. He held it up, looked it over. "Take it," he said. "Don't be stupid."

The *Get Smart* Thermos sits up on my shelf next to a *Battlestar Galactica* Cylon action figure.

AS I WALK into Chicky's house, Chicky is kneeling next to the philodendron, combing through Eve's beige hair with his good fingers as Eve watches *The Operation,* a program where they film an actual operation. Today's is knee surgery. Doctors are driving a nail into a yellow bone. The skin that's cut open and folded back seems plastic, fake. All the bright blood and white tendons make it real. "Come hiking with us," I tell Eve. "You can't sit here and watch this gore all day."

"I talked to Martha," she says, "and it was no misunderstanding. You grabbed her breast."

"It was a misunderstanding in that I thought she wanted me to."

"She didn't, and you're lucky she didn't kick your sorry ass."

"I could take her," I say.

Eve rolls her eyes and focuses again on the operation. Chicky kisses her head.

THERE'S NO RELIEF from the heat in Pima Canyon, but somehow the air is easier to breathe. This time of the year, the mountains are brown and gray, dry as dust, ready to burst into flames and take out a few foothills homes. There are little animal paw prints in the faint, waxy residue on the main stalk of one of the agaves by the trail. I point out the tracks to Chicky.

"Neat," he says. "Let's get moving before those clouds roll in and dump on us."

"It won't rain." The clouds are lurking over the Santa Catalinas as usual. They float there, black, full of water, making our doors and windows stick and the backs of our knees sweat. The clouds seem to dodge the sun, and they shade only the northeast side of town.

We rest in the shadows of cottonwoods and mesquites, lying in the soft sand of an arroyo, eating the sandwiches Eve packed for us. I gather a few dry mesquite pods, snap them, peel back the moist, stringy casing, and flick the hard, black beans at Chicky, who is sleeping. He starts wheezing lightly, and I try to flick the beans into his mouth. He swats them away like flies when they bounce off his face. His yam arm is draped across his chest. He doesn't use it to swat at the beans. It looks like the elbow part bends the wrong way. The skin of his yam arm is pinker than the rest of his body, purple almost, and it's covered in a light fuzz like a baby rabbit.

At first I toss a few beans at his arm, but he doesn't flinch. One of the beans rests on his deformed wrist. Then I poke it lightly with a stick. Nothing. I've been looking at it for months. So I touch it, my heart motoring away in my throat as I do. Chicky's arm is cooler than I thought it would be, and pleasantly soft. I pet it, moving the light fur this way and that, pinching up little clumps of hair, making tiny circus tents out of his skin. I stop when he sniffs deeply and rolls over. His arm flops into the warm sand.

AT WORK TODAY, nothing has changed. I sweat and curse as I pick through the donations. Even though the dark clouds are blocking the sun, I'm wading through shin-burning waves of heat pumping up from the asphalt.

Chicky's working quickly, sorting a box of clothes: jumpers, bibs, and baby-sized shirts and pants—nothing good for him. His face is glazed with sweat and ruddy. Price and Daniel have been lugging furniture all morning. Their muscles bulge and shine. They look like action heroes, lifting heavier and heavier pieces.

At lunch I walk to Magpies Pizza for a slice. The rich kids are panhandling in their usual spot. Today their hair is emergency red-orange. The girl one carries a *Bionic Woman* lunchbox. It's in amazing shape—very little rim wear, clean lithos. The front depicts Jaime Sommers running faster than a car with her bionic German shepherd. I forget the dog's name.

"Where'd you get that?" I ask her. "The lunchbox?" They stink of patchouli.

"Value Village," she says. "Duh."

"Liar."

"I was with her, asshole," the boy one says to me. "It was only a buck."

"I'll give you twenty for it."

"No way," the girl one says. "It's worth way more. It's from like 1977."

On my way back to Val Vil, eating my slice, grease trailing down my wrist and dripping off my elbow, the girl one waves the lunchbox at me. It makes that clinky metal sound like all old lunchboxes do when you swing them around.

Chicky and Price and Daniel aren't back from lunch yet, but I start unloading more of the truck because I have nothing better to do. The first box I grab is light, and when I place it down on the asphalt, I see my mother's handwriting on the top—*Beacon Foundation*—and I freak out for a second until I realize I'm being stupid, that she wrote it, so she's not dead or anything.

Inside are familiar clothes from when I was a kid: my Toros baseball shirt, old jeans and sweaters. My father's turquoise pants. Thick polyester. He wore them with white shoes and a white belt. I remember thinking he looked cool wearing them on the back porch, sitting in the red director's chair, smoking. In a way, he was cool. Relaxed. I hold up a shirt of my mother's: navy blue, with a white rounded collar. I used to call it the Pilgrim Shirt. Next is a denim skirt with an elastic waist. I never called that anything. Most of the rest is nursing uniforms, white and light blue. Both pants and tops. And her old, trashed nursing shoes lie on the bottom of the box like dead things.

AT HOME THIS AFTERNOON, I lie on my couch and wonder about my mother's life change, her getting rid of her uniforms. She called and left a message on my machine last week, but I forgot until I found the box at work today. As I stare at the chipping ceiling, I imagine my mother driving a new car—a red Jeep—to her new job, where she doesn't have to wear those shoes. She has her own air-conditioned office that smells like fresh carpeting. A coffee machine down the hall, a water cooler, free pens. But this is dumb. She's a psych nurse, not even an RN, just an LPN. She probably works at another rehab where the uniforms are different. She takes the bus to work. She got bit again today by a guy my age. Before she goes to bed tonight, she'll dab hydrogen peroxide on the wound and watch it fizz.

So I get in my car and drive over to the hardware store and buy three sizes of screws that look as if they'd be the right ones for my mother's garage door hinge. It's almost six when

I arrive at my mother's, but she's not home. Someone has pulled up the dead saltbush. In its place is a barrel cactus. I squat in the swirls of dust and leaves and lift the garage door.

But I'm too late; someone has already fixed the hinge—it no longer sags. The hot wind is swelling, and I feel a few patters of rain for the first time this summer. The neighbor's palm trees bend in the wind. The dried fronds make loud crumbling noises.

Lightning rips through the sky over the city, burns its mark on my eyes as I watch it from my old spot—a sun-faded director's chair perched on my mother's flat roof. I climb up here whenever it rains, and sit on the wet canvas, taking in the rising smells: first, tarry steam from the driveway, then the creosote dominates, fills my lungs and head, makes me think something substantial is happening and someday I'll understand it.

AS I DRIVE out to Country Club Road this morning, it's still raining, and the brown water is lapping over the curbs. Real rapids in the turning lane. A man whose blue Volvo has stalled in the middle climbs out the passenger window and splashes into the water with his shiny leather shoes. The water is higher than his knees. I want to yell "Duh!" at him, but I've done the same thing. I didn't ruin good shoes, but I have stalled my car in a flooded street.

The water gushing down Tucson Boulevard is deeper, forms bigger white-capped rapids. A tall Chevy four-by-four sits in the humming chocolate-milk waves. People's front lawns are flooded. I get out of my car and stand on a landscape rock just on the edge of the street so I can watch all this. It's drizzling, and the Catalina Mountains are draped in individual dollops of fluffy fog. A mailbox and its wooden stand float by. Lots of cans and cups. Wrappers. Palm fronds and trash bags have gathered at the wheels of the Chevy. A good rain. There are about ten other people doing what I'm doing, standing outside their cars, watching, scratching their heads, wondering how they're getting to work.

"Wow," a man in a suit says. "Wow."

"Wow," I say.

The drizzle stops, and I'm thinking Chicky and Price and Daniel are letting stuff slip through. I hate to think what might end up in the store for customers to buy. Maybe Chicky and Price and Daniel can't get to work. If the Stone and Fourth Avenue underpasses are flooded, Price and Daniel definitely can't make it. If Chicky's there by himself, it's hopeless. I imagine him casually unloading a box of toys from the '60s—Beatles' Flip Your Wig game, *Lost in Space* robot, *Jetsons* lunchbox—all in mint condition, recently retrieved from an elementary school's thirty-year time capsule. The panhandling girl will pay a dollar for the *Jetsons* lunchbox. She'll wave it at me tomorrow when I go for a slice at lunch.

The answering machine's going when I return to my apartment. I listen to my mother leave a message: ". . . you on the roof yesterday, and I'm just calling to see if you're all right. I guess you made it through the flooding and you're at work. Call me back for a change."

I call Val Vil after she hangs up, but no one's answering. Ram is probably eating a hot dog, sitting in an old beanbag chair, sputtering farts, ignoring the phone. Chicky's out back unloading my toys even though he's only allowed to unload clothes. The Nepalese workers are afraid of the phone because they can't speak English. They curse at it in Nepali. I drop the receiver, and I look up at my shelves, my collection, Erik Estrada's plastic face, and listen to the rain begin to batter the roof again.

d_is_gciplinary

September 3, Third Period—Art Concepts,
Linda Hardiman, MFA

Charles Backenbrush licked Brooke Luter's upper arm as she walked by his desk on her way to the trash can. I told him his behavior was inappropriate and offensive. He apologized to Brooke Luter, but later in the period I saw him wag his tongue at her. She laughed in response to his second tongue gesture. I did not comment on it.

September 7, Third Period—Art Concepts,
Linda Hardiman, MFA

Charles Backenbrush lifted his shirt and pressed his right nipple on the ink pad. Then he made nipple prints. I told him to stop, but he continued. He repeated "bird's nest"

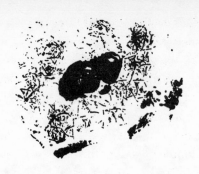

Nipple Print. Charles Backenbrush.

many times until I threatened him with detention. At that point, he asked if he could go to the rest room and clean off his chest. I said, "Yes."

September 14, Third Period—Art Concepts,
Linda Hardiman, MFA
Charles Backenbrush made a vagina out of clay. I balled up the vagina and mashed it. I explained that a vagina was inappropriate. I told him to report to detention today after school.

October 16, Third Period—Art Concepts,
Linda Hardiman, MFA
I told Charles Backenbrush to please clean his area. He said, "Okay, Mrs. Hard-on." I said, "Hardiman." Then he said, "Hard-on ma'am." I told him to go to the office. Then he said, "The orifice?" Then his friend Frederick Lee made a crude gesture with his hands. Frederick Lee made an O out of his thumb and index finger on one hand (I cannot recall if it was his left or right) and stuck his other hand's index finger repeatedly through the O to imitate sexual intercourse. I asked Frederick Lee to go to the office as well. I cited this incident on Frederick Lee's disciplinary log.

November 6, Third Period—Art Concepts,
Linda Hardiman, MFA

I put Charles Backenbrush and Frederick Lee at separate worktables on either end of the room for the clothespin angel project. When I looked over at Charles Backenbrush early in the period, he was licking the hair on his arm. I asked him to stop, and he did. A few minutes later he was licking his arm again. I told him to go to the office and not to make any jokes about the word "office," and if he did make a joke about the word "office," then I would guarantee a week of detention. He laughed and said, "Bird's nest" (a reference to his nipple print of September 7), before leaving.

December 9, Third Period—Art Concepts,
Linda Hardiman, MFA

Charles Backenbrush was looking at a pornographic magazine, *Young Shavers,* which I confiscated and burned in the kiln. He claimed he found it in Mr. Conley's desk in a drawer full of similar magazines. Right after I told him to go to the office, he said Frederick Lee got the magazine from his father's tool bench. Charles Backenbrush then proceeded to name other magazines from the tool bench. I told him to stop, but he loudly named at least six more, each having an offensive title. When Charles Backenbrush left, I asked Frederick Lee if he (Frederick Lee) had brought the magazine to school. He said no, that Charles Backenbrush (he called him by his nickname "Chigger") had gotten it from his mother's boyfriend as payment for helping him fix his truck. He added that his (Frederick Lee's) father was a Christian. I told Frederick Lee to sit down and finish his clothespin angel, which was already one day late. When I later looked at Charles Backenbrush's clothespin angel, which he had left on the table, I saw that it was made to have large breasts (pasta shells and broken-off pencil erasers) and a penis (a painted pen cap with a head of clay).

February 11, Third Period—Art Concepts, Linda Hardiman, MFA

Charles Backenbrush called Brooke Luter a "fat whore" for using the last of the red acrylic paint. I told him to apologize. He did.

March 14, Third Period—Art Concepts, Linda Hardiman, MFA

When I told Charles Backenbrush that he received a B+ on his soft sculpture project, he said, "What the hell!" and stood in a threatening manner (he puffed out his chest and moved his face to within four inches of my face). I explained that his doll was very good but he failed to use at least seven different materials as I had specified. He then proceeded to show me how he used seven different materials: pantyhose (nylon), polyester fiber, yarn (acrylic), glue, string (cotton), paint, and buttons. I told him that I was sorry, that I hadn't taken the polyester fiber into account, and that I would raise his grade. He said, "You better." I said that his tone was inappropriate. He apologized.

March 22, Third Period—Art Concepts, Linda Hardiman, MFA

After I sent Brooke Luter to the office for wearing a tight, cropped T-shirt that exposed her midriff (indicated in Brooke Luter's disciplinary log), Charles Backenbrush stopped working on his painted box and approached my desk. He said students should be able to wear what they want. I said that I agreed, as long as students don't wear anything that might be distracting to others. He said the rule was "bullshit" and that anything could be distracting, even the shirt I was wearing (an oversize sky-blue oxford cloth shirt). I told him that his tone and language were disrespectful to me and his fellow students. He said he couldn't control his language and tone because he was too distracted by my shirt. I sent him to the office.

April 4, Third Period—Art Concepts,
Linda Hardiman, MFA

Charles Backenbrush announced in the middle of our Native American sandpainting project that he thought I was a good teacher. Many students laughed, as if Charles Backenbrush's comment had been sarcastic. I told the class that sort of interruption was disruptive and counterproductive. He said he really meant what he said and he wasn't trying to be funny. I suggested we all focus on Native American sandpainting again.

April 11, Third Period—Art Concepts,
Linda Hardiman, MFA

Charles Backenbrush carved a nude large-breasted woman into his linoleum. Below it he carved the name "Brooke." He made prints from the linoleum before I noticed the design. I told him that his prints were hurtful and rude and that he should apologize to Brooke Luter. He said millions of artists draw or paint nude women. I told him he was right but not in eighth-grade art class and not of classmates without their consent. He accused me of stopping him from being creative. I said his tone was disrespectful and inappropriate, and he apologized to me and to Brooke Luter. Then he asked if he could have his linoleum back so he could carve away Brooke Luter's name. I said the large-breasted woman was still inappropriate. He then declared

Linoleum Prints. Charles Backenbrush.

that women's breasts are beautiful. I agreed but said they are beautiful in the appropriate settings. He said he thought they were always beautiful, in any setting. I said that his opinion was okay, but not everyone thinks so.

May 3, Third Period—Art Concepts,
Linda Hardiman, MFA

Charles Backenbrush brought a portable stereo with earphones to class today. I told him that portable stereos are not allowed on campus and asked him to bring the portable stereo to the office until the end of the day. He said he would, and he left. During break I checked with Marla Woods and Diane Beckman in the main office, and both said that Charles Backenbrush had not been in the main office today. They also said that no one had dropped off a portable stereo for Charles Backenbrush today. I assigned

Charles Backenbrush to detention for tomorrow afternoon (Tuesday, May 4).

June 3, Third Period—Art Concepts, Linda Hardiman, MFA

Frederick Lee covered his hand with glue and chased Charles Backenbrush around the workstations. I told Frederick Lee to stop chasing Charles Backenbrush and to wash his hand. He said that he didn't have to listen to me because it was the last day of school, and he continued to chase Charles Backenbrush. He dripped glue on the floor in many areas of the room. I told him to go to the office, and he laughed at me and wiped his gluey hand on my desk. At that point, Charles Backenbrush grabbed Frederick Lee's wrist and said, "Go to the office, bitch." Frederick Lee did go to the office. I reported this incident in Frederick Lee's disciplinary log. I told Charles Backenbrush that his grabbing Frederick Lee and calling him a "bitch" was disrespectful and rude. He said he was sorry. I told him that I would like to speak to him after class, and I began to wipe up Frederick Lee's glue mess. After class ended, Charles Backenbrush remained seated at his workstation. I sat down across from him and told him that I greatly admired the coil pot he had glazed earlier in the week, and that I hoped he would continue taking art classes in high school next year. I also mentioned that I hoped his behavior would improve over the summer so it wouldn't hinder his artistic growth like it had this year. He reached across the table and took my hand in his. He kissed the top of my hand lightly and kept holding it. We sat like that through break until the fourth-period bell rang.

m_co_hn_ok_we y

WE'RE HUNGRY, REALLY HUNGRY. I'm licking the MSG residue off the inside of an empty Doritos bag, and Sally's eating a heel of bread sprayed with butter-flavored Pam. We've made a vow not to spend any of our money—$127 between the three of us—unless it's absolutely necessary. We'll need it when the car breaks down. At least that's what Tuck says.

"Why the hell do you have this stuff in your van?" Sally asks Tuck. She waves the can of Pam. Tuck doesn't respond. He pretends he isn't hungry and ignores us, concentrating on the road instead. Three hundred miles ago, he told us that hunger is all in the mind. We're in his van, forty-one hours into our trip, speeding down Highway 44 on our way to Joshua Tree.

Sally's holding out, though. Yesterday, after being caught

stealing a box of doughnuts and enduring a lecture from a fat 7-Eleven manager, she vowed never to steal food again until we each did it ourselves two more times.

"But Sally, it's the age and gender thing," I say.

"Suck my age and gender thing, Brett," she tells me.

"If you get caught, you get yelled at. If Tuck or me gets caught, we go to jail and get raped on an hourly basis."

"Then you two can eat shit," she says.

She's actually justified. It is our turn to steal the food. Technically, it's my turn. Sally stole a loaf of bread, peanut butter, Doritos, a box of crackers, and dozens of Snickers— her favorite. She's good at it. Tuck had ripped off almost as much, including a cheesecake from the bakery section of a huge supermarket, as we first crossed into Oklahoma. Up until now, I've only stolen a package of stale generic fig bars.

Tuck looks back. "It's your turn, man. Not that my hunger is anything more than slightly visceral, but it's your turn, man," he says.

"Yeah, asshole," Sally says. Her lips are puckered because of the butter-flavored Pam. She looks like she's posing for a lipstick ad. She could, she's cute enough.

"I know. Shut up. Pull over at the next place," I say.

"THINK. WHEN YOU'RE on the rocks, think of it as being on a leash," Tuck said, pointing to his head. "Gravity holds the leash, and you have to dupe gravity to get where you want. You can never outmuscle gravity, but it's possible to use chicanery to get where you want to be."

I was clinging to the south wall of the K mart, about three feet off the ground, moving sideways. A typical Saturday night. We often met there after I finished my shift at the Sonic Burger and Tuck was relieved of his baby-sitting duties. Bricks on the K mart wall jutted out here and there, making it the best warm-up wall in Lebanon, Missouri—not too easy to make it from the east edge of the wall to the west edge, even challenging in some parts.

Lebanon's not known for its rock climbing, so we made do with what we had. I met Tuck one night while I was climbing the sloped roof of the Li'l Kids nursery school. He parked his trashed van next to the swing set and started doling out advice from his car: "Bend your knees more, and stick out your butt. Your legs have to be what's holding you to the wall, not your arms." Then he got out of his van and began scaling the roof himself.

Back then he was much better than me at all aspects of climbing, especially footwork. I had the shoes, though. I ordered them from the classifieds of *Outside*—dense, smooth soles and blue leather uppers. They set me back $125. If I hadn't been wearing the shoes, he probably never would have stopped that night at the nursery school.

Sally worked at the K mart where we climbed. That's how we met her. She stayed and watched us some nights, making fun of us, calling us wannabe climbers. "You try it," we used to say, and one night she did. She liked it and was actually pretty good.

She got to be a skilled climber about the third time we took her out. We went to Li'l Kids one night because she wanted more of a challenge than the K mart wall could offer. We set up ropes, and Tuck belayed her from below. She was tied into the rope with her new harness, and Tuck dealt with the slack from his sitting position in the sand of the playground, even though the peak of the Li'l Kids roof was only about twenty feet off the ground. She had the form down instantly, always using her legs—she had to; her arms were too wimpy.

"There's a good hold to your right, up about three feet," Tuck said.

"Shut up," Sally said. She reached for that hold.

"Now step up with your left foot, there's a little ledge there near your knee."

"Shut up," Sally repeated. She stepped up with her left leg.

I don't know why we let her climb with us in the beginning. I mean, she was a little snot, even then. She was cute as hell, though—a sixteen-year-old blond cheerleader with the mouth of a drunken sailor. She squirreled away everything she earned at K mart, and about the fifth time we picked her up, she had her own climbing shoes and all the equipment we could possibly use—ten or so caribiners, two new ropes, harnesses, belay devices, everything—and all of it brand new. She ordered it from REI through the mail, squandering her savings in one shot.

Tuck used to have to baby-sit his grandmother forty hours a week. It was a pretty good deal. He did that, and his parents let him live at home and gave him a twenty-five-dollar-a-week allowance. He said he felt weird getting allowance at his age—twenty-seven—but he got free food and car insurance, too. His grandmother was harmless, the victim of a few strokes. She used to be a speed reader, a disciple of Evelyn Wood's, so all she did besides watch TV was read those *Reader's Digest*s with the oversize print. Of course Tuck had to turn the pages for her. He read what she read—he acquired his extensive vocabulary from the "It Pays to Enrich Your Word Power" section of each issue. Sometimes he'd use a word, and I'd have no idea what he was saying. His favorite was *atavistic*. Even after I asked him what it meant and looked it up in the dictionary, I still didn't really understand it. I still don't.

It was tough for Tuck to get days off, so I was excited

when he said his grandmother was going to stay with his aunt in Springfield for the whole month of June.

We didn't actually want to bring Sally. I mean, we knew she'd be a challenge to travel with, especially with no money and in Tuck's trashed van. We tried to keep it a secret from her, but she found out and threatened to kill us if we didn't let her come. I think Tuck felt guilty—she did buy all that equipment, and she never would have had the urge to climb if it wasn't for us. We had to bring her along. We took off for Joshua Tree three days ago—a week after Sally's school got out. She made up an elaborate lie for her parents. She's supposed to be up in Canada at her friend Vivi's uncle's lake-side cabin. Tuck called her dad, pretending to be Vivi's uncle. He even gave him the real phone number of some resort up there with a funny Canadian prefix.

Tuck pulls the van into a Snatch and Scram parking lot. We're in Sapulpa, Oklahoma, he tells us. He parks to the side, so the clerk can't see the van.

"You better get something good," Sally tells me, "like Snickers, or I'll castrate you."

"Get something salubrious," Tuck adds.

"I'll get what I get," I say.

There are only a few other people in the store, some kids buying baseball cards, a skinny woman asking for matches. I head toward the cold drinks in the back and pretend to be deciding on one until the kids bring their purchases up to the counter.

When they're all up there, counting out their change, I make my move. I rub up against the shelves in the fridge and stuff a Coke down my Jockeys—it's cold, real cold. I take another, the bargain brand this time—Snatch and Scram Cola. I'll pay for that one with my last bit of secret change. I look back at the counter at the last kid getting his cards. I grab the closest thing off the shelf to my right—a can of Spam—and I stuff it down the back of my Jockeys. It's not as cold, and it's a bit more secure than the Coke up front, which I can feel easing its way out a leg hole. I walk to the counter sort of crouched and limping, like I'm trying to hide a boner.

The clerk rings up the cheapo cola, tapping the keys of the register with her hooked red fingernails. "Forty-one," she says. She's reading a confession magazine with a photo of a gagged woman on the front, and she doesn't even look up at me. I hand her a quarter, a nickel, a dime, and a penny, and I make for the exit. The Coke slips all the way out of my underwear before I reach the door. I catch it through my pants, down almost at the knee. The clerk doesn't look up from her magazine, and I finally make it outside.

"What'd you get?" Sally asks.

"Two Cokes and a can of Spam." I pull the can out from the back of my underwear.

"Great, now we have Pam and Spam," she says. "Thanks a lot, asshole."

"I'll take it," Tuck says. He peels back the lid of the can, dumps out the jelly-packed Spam onto the dash, lifts it to his face, and takes a big bite out of it. "Better than ham. Less fat."

Sally takes the real Coke, and I'm left with the bargain crap that tastes like metal.

SEVEN HOURS LATER, we're approaching Amarillo. Tuck says we're going to stop for the night just west of the city. My mouth tastes like shit. I had to siphon gas, which has become my official job now that they've determined I suck at stealing food. It's eight at night, and Sally wakes up.

"Find a K mart in Amarillo," she says.

"Why?" Tuck asks.

"Do you want to eat or what?" she says.

We stop at a gas station as we reach the outskirts of Amarillo. Sally leans her head out the window and asks the guy where there's a K mart.

"There's a Target about six miles down this road, and a Wal-Mart just a few miles if you take a right at that intersection," he says.

Sally looks at the patch on his shirt. It says FRANK. "Look, Frank, we need a K mart. Where's a K mart?"

"The K mart's much farther away than the Wal-Mart and the Target," he says.

"Are you deaf? Where the hell's the K mart? Not the Wal-Mart or the Target. The K mart," she says.

He tells her to fuck off and suck his dick. Tuck and I laugh. We drive a bit down the road to a phone booth and look up the address—easy to find with the map in the front of the phone book.

We get to the parking lot of the K mart, and Sally rummages through her bag.

"What time is it?" she asks Tuck.

"Eight-forty-eight," he says.

"Well, I've got twelve minutes to provide for you losers. Assuming, of course, that all K marts close at nine." She pulls her K mart uniform out of her bag. The SALLY name tag is still on it. "Don't look, pathetic perverts," she says as she begins to slide into the red and blue uniform. I peek, and I think Tuck does, too—he uses the rearview mirror. She disappears into the store.

Ten minutes later, she emerges with two bags of food. "I don't know why I do this for you fuckers, but here." She empties the bags into the backseat. Food, mostly junk food because that's all you can really buy at K mart, spills over the seat. There must be thirty Snickers. She looks at me: "And you better suck some gas while we're stopped."

I find an old Volkswagen parked near the Dumpsters in back of the building and start the siphon. This time I don't get any gas directly in my mouth—I've gotten better at it—but still the fumes taste almost as bad. I manage to siphon a few gallons. At least Sally got some root beer to wash the taste out of my mouth.

IT'S STILL DARK—4:27 A.M.—but we're moving. I guess Tuck was inspired and couldn't sleep. There aren't many lights around, no buildings, but every once in a while a car passes us.

"How long have we been driving?" I ask him.

"I woke up at three," he says. "We'll need more fuel in about an hour," he tells me.

"Great."

Sally's asleep, quietly wheezing, and I have to piss. I use a soda can, almost fill it, and toss it out the window. The wind noise from the window causes Sally to stir. ". . . Stupid fuck," she mumbles. She starts her faint, wheezy snoring again.

"I want to be in Flagstaff this afternoon," Tuck says. "I read that there are some amazing cliffs right outside of town. We can boulder around and set up some easy belays."

"Cool," I say. I move up to the passenger seat and play with the radio. All I get are talk and country stations: *Contact your local chapter of the American Honky-Tonk Bar Association . . .* I fall asleep.

"WAKE UP, we need gas," Sally says. She pulls my hair.

"Leave me alone." My cheek's wet with drool, and I wipe it on my sleeve.

"Wake up, we need gas," she whines. "No gas, no food for you. And I still have plenty from the K mart heist."

"I'm up," I say.

Tuck pulls into a huge truck stop. It has everything: two restaurants, a convenience store, showers, a Laundromat, a western clothing shop. He parks next to a van similar to his—just as trashed, blocking us from a view of people in the truck stop. I get out, still half asleep, and begin the siphon. No gas in my mouth. I fill three milk gallon jugs and dump them into Tuck's tank.

"You smell like gas," Sally says as I get back in the van.

"Shut up. I'm sick of your shit," I say. "Tuck, did you ever consider that these people I steal gas from could be just as broke as we are?"

"They can siphon their own gas," Sally says. "Fuck them."

"No, fuck you," I tell her.

She finally shuts up.

FLAGSTAFF SEEMS LIKE it's all motels. There are hundreds of them, all with dumb names and cheap rates: the Wagon Wheel with free HBO for twenty-two, the Flying Carpet Inn with free continental breakfast for twenty . . . Sally relentlessly complains about our BO and her dirty hair until Tuck gives in. We spend eighteen dollars on a room at the Canyon Motel with two double beds and an ugly painting of a bowl of fruit. I'd love a bowl of fruit.

None of us takes a shower or anything, not even Sally; we want to get out to the cliffs that Tuck has been raving about, before it gets dark. Tuck calls a sporting goods store, and we get directions. "The cliffs are only about three miles from where we are," he tells us. "Out past the Purina plant."

WE PULL UP next to a few cars at the end of a dirt road. There's a mountain, a steep mountain, mostly white rock bluffs, right in our faces. Tuck gets this crazed look in his eyes, a look I've never seen. He starts to jog ahead of Sally and me.

We find him at the end of the trail with his cheek up against a beautiful granite rock face. It looks like he's trying to hug it. Sally gasps and immediately starts to climb around.

There are other groups of climbers out there, some tied into belays, others just bouldering around like Sally. One guy is attempting an overhang about twenty feet up, listening to another guy belaying him from below: "There's a great hold about a foot above your right hand. You're gonna have to go for it." The guy reaches for it and falls, penduluming at the end of the rope. "Shit," he says. The belayer laughs and slowly lets him down.

Tuck is now rubbing the rock wall like a blind man reading a Braille billboard.

I join Sally. She's talking to some British guys.

"We've been out here for two weeks, and we still haven't exhausted all the climbs," one of them says. And they do look like they've been out here for weeks: scraggly beards, matted hair, and sun-crisped faces. Their colorful climbing clothes look dingy.

"Will one of you guys belay me?" Sally asks. "I've got my harness here, and I could just tie into your setup."

"Sure, snap in," one of the guys says. He's sizing Sally up, staring at her ass.

"On belay," she says.

"Belay on."

"Climbing."

"Climb."

She follows a crack up the face, inserting her tiny hands and leaning back as she climbs. She makes it up about thirty feet and rests on a little ledge, feet dangling over. The guy belaying her, Miles, advises her about the rest of the climb— there's no more crack for her to use, and she's got about twenty feet to go. Miles's climbing buddy, Nigel, sits next to me on the ground.

"She's pretty good," Nigel says.

"She is," I say.

"Where have you climbed before?"

"Nowhere really. Just buildings in Missouri."

"Really? Her, too?" he asks.

"Yup."

"Have some MC if you'd like." He takes a lid off a coffee can. It's full of fruity-smelling brown kibble. I grab a handful and start munching. It tastes like granola, only there's no cinnamon and its texture is uniform. It's slightly sour, and I can taste banana and citrus.

"What is this?" I ask.

"Monkey Chow," Nigel says.

"Not like Cat Chow?"

"Yes, like Cat Chow. You can buy it at the Purina plant. We bought a fifty-pound bag and took it down to Joshua Tree. That's all we ate."

I crunched some more. "How much for a bag?"

"Only eleven dollars—that's the beauty of it. You saw the plant when you drove out here?"

"Yeah, we passed it."

Tuck calls me to help him set up a belay. He's hiked around and is already on top of the cliff. The belay is almost ready to go. The rope he throws down gets snagged in a bush. I untangle it, and he comes down. He's first. I belay him. As he starts, he still has that wild look, only now he's sort of crying, with a sickening, almost perverse grin.

THE SUN FINALLY SETS—we all got a lot of climbing in, and we're exhausted and starving, sitting on the beds in the motel, eating the remains of the Amarillo K mart heist. We're down to a few cans of soda and some flavorless corn chips. I gaze at the ugly, faded picture of the fruit.

"You know, those guys Miles and Nigel eat Monkey Chow," I say.

"What the hell's Monkey Chow?" Sally asks.

"You were eating it," I say. "That brown stuff in the cof- fee can. It's only eleven dollars for a fifty-pound bag."

"I'd eat roadkill for that price," Tuck says. He goes into the bathroom to take a long-overdue shower.

"We should get some. You guys wouldn't have to steal as much, and it really doesn't taste that bad. You just have to forget what it's called," I say.

"I'd rather steal good stuff," Sally says.

"You ate more of it than I did."

"I didn't know what it was," she says. "Besides, I can steal whatever we need. You just keep providing the gas."

. . .

WE DECIDE TO stay in Flagstaff for a few more days. We camp in Tuck's van as usual—our one night of comfort and hygiene in the motel ends quickly. Sally stole everything from the motel room—she even unbolted the still life, so now I can gaze at the fruit bowl while we're driving. The artist's name is Jay Lazora. I wonder what he would think if he saw his painting in the back of the van next to all our ropes, hardware, and a bunch of gas-stinky plastic milk jugs. I'm actually sort of glad she took it. I've learned to really like it.

We pass the Purina plant. There's a big red and white checkerboard on a watershed.

"We really should invest eleven dollars in fifty pounds of food," I say.

"You just worry about the gas, and I'll worry about the food," Sally says. "Didn't I feed you well this morning?"

"Besides, we need the money if this van breaks down," Tuck says.

Sally starts bouldering around as soon as we get to the face of the bluffs. We're the first ones out here, so Tuck and I set up our belay near a great overhang. I go first.

"Remember the gravity-leash theory," Tuck tells me as I tie in.

"That doesn't work on overhangs," I tell him.

"Yes, it does."

The first twenty feet are pretty easy, like stairs, sloped the right way. The overhang starts now. In order to look up for holds, I have to bend my head way back. I can't really see any places to grab, and my right leg is shaking like a sewing machine needle.

"Up to your right, about two feet, it looks like there's something you can grab," Tuck yells.

I press with my shaking leg and reach up. I grab a hold of a lip substantial enough to sustain my weight, but there's nowhere to put my legs or my other hand. I fall back, I see Tuck, I swing and dangle and see the rock right before I bash my face. Tuck lets me down slowly. I have a bloody nose and a burning scrape on my chin.

"Cool," he says. "Battle scars. Gravity won this round."

"Shut up," I say.

Sally comes over and laughs at me.

AT AROUND NOON, Sally and I complain of hunger. Tuck doesn't want to take down the belay—none of us has made it past the overhang, although Sally was close on her second attempt.

"We'll lose our spot," he says.

"Who the hell cares? We'll never make it," Sally says.

"We might," he says.

"I'll stay," I say. "I'll watch the equipment."

"No, I'll stay," he says, and he throws me the keys.

"We could save a lot of time if we just buy that fifty-pound bag of Monkey Chow," I say.

Sally wants to find another K mart, so I pull over at the first gas station we see, to get directions. She's polite this time, and we get directions right away.

"See where a little courtesy gets you," I tell her as we drive down the main strip toward the K mart.

"Lick me," she says.

WE PULL INTO the parking lot. "I'll be quick," she says. She already has her uniform on. "Any requests?"

"Anything but candy bars and soda," I say.

She disappears into the store. I look across the parking lot. To the north are huge peaks, the San Francisco Peaks. Dumb name, considering they're about seven hundred miles from San Francisco, but amazing. One is still snow-capped. A woman is yelling at her little girl two cars away: "I told you not to take off the top! Look at this sticky shit!" I hear a smack and then the girl crying. I unroll the window and rubberneck. The woman is holding her little girl out in front of her by the armpits, letting orange soda drip off her pink overalls onto the parking lot. The girl is wriggling, barely breathing between sobs, face almost purple. The woman sees me gawking. "What the hell you looking at?" I turn away and switch on the radio. It's Whitney Houston, bellowing, but I turn it up anyway.

It's been more than thirty minutes, and Sally's not out yet. I get a little worried, so I go into the store to look for her. It's big, spacious, and organized, but I don't see her in any of the food aisles. I go back out to the car, thinking maybe I missed her, but she's not there either. I go back in and ask a woman at the big red customer-service desk to page her.

A man comes out from behind a blue door and whispers something to the woman who paged Sally. "Do you want to come back here?" he asks, pointing at me.

"Why?"

"Sally's back there. We caught her trying to leave without paying for a few items."

"I can't. I'll go call her mother," I say. I start almost running toward the door, then realize I'm almost running and slow down.

"YOU JUST LEFT her there?" Tuck asks. He's taking down the belay from the choice spot with the overhang.

"What was I supposed to do, tell the guy I was waiting in the getaway car?"

"I don't know, let me think," he says.

We both think. My mind races. Me in jail. Sally at home, grounded. We don't say much on the way over to the K mart. We sit in the parking lot. Tuck mumbles something about aiding and abetting and juveniles and crossing state lines. I'm thinking the same stuff, looking up at the San Franciscos. I'm hungry as hell. If I moved, I'd faint or dry-heave. I can't even look at the painting in the backseat. I'm sure Tuck's hungry, too. Finally, he sighs and says, "Let's go buy some Monkey Chow," and we drive off toward the Purina plant.

Ira_o j_azona

WE WERE CHEAP-ASS PERVERTS, Beezer and me. We'd go
down to Nogales and get tanked on fifty-cent Mexican beer
outside the liquor stores, sitting at rickety tin card tables set
up on the sidewalk. The blanket-and-sombrero-toting tourists would stroll by us: new walking shoes, faraway-college
sweatshirts, windbreakers, cameras. Their eager-eyed kids
would clutch illegal fireworks that they'd stuff in their tube
socks to sneak over the border. They all looked too clean and
bright for the brown, humid smudge of Nogales.

After we got good and drunk, we'd saunter over to the
strip places—¡Ladies Bars!—in La Zona Roja, where they
sold the same Pacifico beer for three dollars a bottle. We'd
buy one each and sit and gawk at the women onstage like
any other run-of-the-mill lechers; only we were in Mexico
and inebriated, so it seemed like being there at the Ladies

Bars was almost required and somehow the most natural thing in the world.

That night the strippers were sad-eyed, like mothers of troubled children—and one of them *was* a mother, because when she squished around her doughy breasts, she shot milk in my friend Beezer's eye. The same woman snatched my John Deere cap right off my head and danced around with it like it was all hers, rubbing it seductively over her body and finally putting it on top of her sprayed-up, crispy bangs. A cowboy turned to me and said, "That was a good hat," like he understood my loss. It was a good hat: shaped to fit my big skull, perfectly molded bill, and it smelled right— like minty dandruff shampoo and sweaty wool.

THE MILK-SQUIRTING HAT-GRABBER left the stage, and I sat there, convinced that my hat was gone for good, tossed on the floor of the dancers' cramped changing room, hidden under a velvet pull-away skirt next to some forlorn go-go boots.

"It's a good way to lose a hat," Beezer said to me, taking a fake sip from his beer, sniffing, and wiping his nose on his sleeve. He had snorted a little mound of crude speed he'd bought for five bones from a shaky street kid as soon as we crossed the border. A stoner we knew from high school— Flynn—had gotten Beezer into that shit while I was back east at college. Beezer didn't have a brother or parents like mine, so he didn't know any better. Beezer was thirty, but he sometimes looked fifteen, especially when he was drunk and wired. That night his face was ruddy and stupid.

I had serious hat-head, so I ran my fingers through my hair and fluffed it up. I knew Becky, my girlfriend at the time, would be happy that my hat was gone. She hated that hat, said it made me look like a Billy Bob.

A less enthusiastic woman trudged out onstage, dancing off-beat to an obnoxious techno version of "Cotton-Eyed Joe" and looking into space with her tired, wide-set eyes. At first she was dressed like a cowgirl, but soon her breasts were sagging out for us, swaying loosely in our faces. Beezer was into her. He kissed one of those breasts and stuffed a dollar in her white boot. At the end of her routine, she was a nasty bandita, shooting cap guns into the audience, wearing nothing but a vinyl holster.

We each ordered another beer, mollifying the grumpy waiter. It was around one in the morning, and the place was stinky with dusty ranchers and locals who had finished selling their wares to gringos. I wanted to leave, but then I saw my hat again, this time on a different stripper. She rode a dingy white donkey onto the stage, and the whole crowd started howling, whooping it up. I was wondering, Am I really so pathetic that I'll sit here and watch a woman fuck around with a donkey on the slight chance that I'll get my cap back? I decided, No, I'm not, and I tapped Beezer on the shoulder.

He turned around. "Your hat," he said. Then he looked back to the stripper. She was lying under the donkey, pulling on its pink dingus, getting it ready.

"Let's go," I yelled in Beezer's ear. "Now, man!"

Beezer was usually good that way. He would listen most of the time. He was dense, but he knew it, so he paid attention to me. I'd saved his ass on way too many occasions.

But that night he didn't listen—he was all speeded up and fidgety. He stumbled over guys and chairs and hopped onstage, and as he squatted down to grab my hat off the stripper's head, the donkey reared back and kicked him in the temple.

The way Beezer's eyes looked, loose and rolled white as cue balls, I thought he was dead. The stripper sprang out from under the donkey and jumped up, her hands glistening with oil in the pulsating stage lights. She laughed vengefully above the sexy, jazzy foreplay music when she saw Beezer on his back. The donkey remained unaffected by the whole thing, not even snorting or moving his cloudy eyes, just twitching his ass muscles and shaking his tail a little.

As I pushed through whores and slobs and tables to get to the stage, Beezer stood up. "I got your hat, man," he said, clutching it in victory like he had just captured the flag. His left eye was still stuck white. It didn't roll back to normal.

THE CUSTOMS OFFICER at the border looked twice at Beezer and that eye. "You all right?"

"Fine," Beezer said. "I'm an American citizen, and I have nothing to declare except that I'm drunk, and so is Sam here."

"Shut the hell up," I told Beezer. Border cops had scared me since I was a kid and my brother Brian made me smuggle a dime bag of Mexican ditch weed in my underpants. I was pegged in a second—I was too nervous, and before I knew it, a short, fat officer with thick hairs sprouting from his nostrils was sticking his stubby fingers up my eight-year-old ass. The whole ordeal cost my parents $1,200, but they thought it was funny. It was something to tell their Jacuzzi friends at the club.

I started to worry about Beezer. The damn eye was still rolled back, only now his whole face was glazed over with a sudden flow of moisture. No bruise or cut from the hoof in the head—just the weeping white eye. I told him to blink as we walked to my truck, which was parked a few blocks in on the Arizona side.

"What?"

"Blink."

"Why?" he said.

"Your eye, man. Blink, for God's sake."

It was tough to drive that dull stretch of I-19 back to Tucson at night, drunkish, with Beezer sitting next to me. That eye—I couldn't help glancing over at it. Its moistness caught all the lights, twinkled even. It looked like a zombie's eye. "Beezer, we have to get that eye fixed," I said.

"I don't have insurance anymore," he said. "It won't be stuck tomorrow."

"I hope not."

"I've been kicked in the head much harder," he said before he clicked on the radio to a bouncy pop song.

"What the hell?" I said. "Turn that off now."

I COULD SEE through the kitchen window that Becky was still up, sitting at the table, angrily smoking with a stack of glossy art books spread out in front of her. "Let me guess," she said when I pushed open the screen door, "you were out with Beezer, you're drunk, and you smell like seedy bars."

"Sorry," I said. "All three are true." I took off my hat and looked at it so I didn't have to look at her. There was a small stain on the top, which caused me to wonder why I had been so hasty to put it on my head after getting it back from the strippers.

"Beezer's a dirt-eating hick," she said. "Why don't you just live with him? You obviously prefer his company."

"Look, I said I was sorry."

"He's trash." She sucked hard on her cigarette and flipped

a page in her book. She spread her fingers over a Botero painting of a round boy in a sailor suit. The boy carried a Bible and a candle, and there were two little devils flying over his shoulder. I knew Botero too well—Becky was writing her dissertation on him: *The Sensuality of Plump.* She had been working on it for three years. "The thing I don't get," she continued, "is how you can stand being around such a cretin."

"He's a good guy," I said. "Always has been."

I went over and lifted her hair from her neck and tried to kiss her. She had the kind of hair you could hide in: long and thick and always clean despite her smoking. She pulled away and nearly burned my chin with her cigarette before I could even get a whiff of the familiar citrus fragrance of her shampoo.

"You're sweating out your beer, and you stink," she said. "But I guess I'm lucky tonight. You decided to actually come home."

"Beezer hurt his eye real bad."

"Good." She slammed the book shut and went into the bedroom.

That night I woke up humping an afghan—acrylic, kind of fuzzy. Becky didn't stir, even though I was rocking the bed pretty hard. I could have stopped if I'd been coherent enough to want to—I was about three pumps away from coming—but I didn't, I had already reached that electric part, and I came all over the bed, not even knowing what I had been dreaming.

I wasn't sure how much later it was, but Becky was screaming at me and swatting my head. She was crying and looked like a sea monster with her bugged eyes, her arms flailing, and her light-brown hair mussed and suffused with the early yellow light.

"I can't control wet dreams," I told her. "That's impossible."

"You can't control anything."

I FIRST MET Becky at Dirtbags, a preppy bar near the U of A—walls crammed with black-and-white photos of old baseball teams, and oars, even though there was nowhere to row within a three-hundred-mile radius. As soon as Becky found out that I had graduated from Williams College, she clung to me like a chigger. I tried to tell her that the only reason I went there was because I sacked quarterbacks better than the average smart person. I tried to tell her how I had to earn almost half my college credits at Arizona during the summers because taking a full load at Williams was too much for me, but she wouldn't listen. She pegged me for a smart guy, and that was that. When I said I worked construction, she claimed she knew the type: blue-collar worker by day, poet and philosopher by night.

Beezer was with me at Dirtbags that time, and after Becky squeezed her way into our booth, she asked him where he had gone to college.

"I didn't," he said. "I barely made it out of high school."

She ignored him for the rest of the night. If I'd been wearing my John Deere cap, she never would have spoken to me in the first place, never would have misjudged me as a poet or a philosopher.

Even back then when we were first dating, Becky hated it when I went out with Beezer. For revenge she'd go to the bars she knew Beezer and I frequented—the Round-Up, the Buffet, Bill Tester's Bushwhacker Lounge—and she'd find some slob to make out with. I'd walk in, and there she'd be, tongue-wrestling with the guy in that drunken, slow-motion way, like she knew people were watching. I'd ignore her, sit down at the bar, and pound Coors with Beezer, keeping him out of trouble. She'd leave with her catch, making sure to swagger by me and squeeze his ass. I made a point not to give a shit most of the time.

SO THE MORNING after Beezer got kicked in the head and his eye got stuck, I found this note from Becky:

> Sam—Throw the sheets and blankets in the washing machine. Please don't go out with Beezer tonight. We really need to talk about a few things. I'll be home early.
> Love, Becky

The few things she wanted to talk about were the same few things she always wanted to talk about: my drinking, and Beezer's being a bad influence. I should have cleaned the house like a madman, gone out and bought her some wine and flowers, and had dinner ready for her when she got home. She would have forgiven me and probably wouldn't have brought up those few things for another week. But I didn't want to be forgiven at that point, and I was too hungover and lazy to clean the house or do anything productive except throw the bedding into the washing machine.

I had forgotten how funny and cool she could be, and how she only wanted me to make something of myself. She was the one who coached me through my contractor's exam for months, sitting at the kitchen table flipping through stacks of flash cards. I flunked the exam twice, but she kept helping me.

The night before my third try, she said, "The real world is not multiple choice. That test is a travesty."

"I have to pass."

"You'll pass. Three's a charm."

I flunked again—another eighty-dollar testing fee down the tubes. She knew I was depressed and feeling stupid, so she brought me photocopies of articles about multiple intelligences and learning styles. "You're a kinesthetic learner," she said. "Your kinesthetic IQ is genius-level. You'll be an excellent contractor someday." I was slumped over the table, and she started working my back like a masseuse, rolling her knuckles along my shoulders and giving me karate chops every once in a while.

"Two of Beezer's brothers passed it, and one of them was in special-ed classes in high school," I mumbled.

"That just proves how stupid the test is," she said. "You have a degree from one of the best colleges in the country. You have to remember that."

She taught me a lot—mostly about Botero. I loved listening to her. One night she gave me a whole lecture about fat people in art. "Rubens," she said, "*he* revered corpulence for reasons much different from Botero's."

"I like Rubens," I said. "Sometimes I want to stick my hand in his paintings and poke the fat ladies."

"I don't think that was the kind of aesthetic appreciation Rubens was after," she said, smiling like she knew I had really thought about Rubens's fat beauties. "But Botero would love that sort of response to his paintings. Honest. He has a sense of humor. . . ."

She should have gone to Williams, not me.

I MOVED OVER to Beezer's place that morning. I thought I'd only stay a few days, give Becky a chance to miss me and me to miss her. I scrawled *back in three or four days* on the bottom of the note she left for me. When I returned, I'd tell her I'd go back to Dr. Kilbinski or another shrink if she wanted.

I realized I had forgotten my hat when I pulled into Beezer's driveway, and sweat drips stung my eye. There was no way I was going back for it—Becky was probably home from school, having a conniption about my note and about my forgetting to hang the blankets and sheets out on the line. I was scared for a second, thinking it was Becky's big chance to get rid of my hat. I imagined her cutting it up with garden shears, and tossing the shreds in the trash. Becky destroying my hat, I thought, was a bad way of retiring it. A stripper stealing it would have been much better.

Beezer lived in a crumbling adobe place way out west of town on a dirt road in a forest of saguaros. His grand-mother left it to him when she died; she chose to leave it to him over his three brothers, and his brothers were pissed. It was a creepy place because Beezer never disposed of his grandmother's gewgaws: collectors' plates, figurines, faded velvet paintings of clowns and kittens. But I roomed there because he let me, sleeping up in a little square loft on a musty Navajo rug, squeezed between boxes of Christmas ornaments.

It stayed rolled back, his eye did, for days after he was kicked, so he wore big aviator sunglasses everywhere—looked like a cop with something to prove. I had called "Ask a Nurse" as soon as I saw his eye was still stuck, and the woman told me he needed medical attention right away. I told Beezer, and he told me to shut up. "I got this," he said, holding up a tube of eye ointment. "It won't get infected with this shit in it, and I thought it might help it slide back to normal."

"That's not for eye problems like yours."

"Just give it a few more days," he said. "Like I said, I've been kicked much harder before."

For money, Beezer broke broncs or taught vacationers from the East how to ride and rope. He was good. He could rope calves in competition like he was plucking weeds from sand—easily, methodically, with a stony face. The problem was that his work wasn't steady, especially with a bad eye, so he spent too much time in front of *Ricki Lake* or the Spice sex channel with a Coors in his hand—at least he did while I was staying at his place. I'd wake up at five or so to get to the site, and I'd find him passed out in the orange glow of some third-rate porno. His head would be tilted sideways, and his shirt would be wet with drool, and in the background there'd be exaggerated erotic moans and slurps from the TV. Sometimes his left lid would be peeled back, and I'd see his white eye drying out. I'd go over there and push the lid down, but it would snap back up like it was made of rubber. I'd scramble around for the damn ointment, even though I knew it didn't help any, then I'd squirt a blob on my finger and dab it into that eye. I had to. It was my hat he had saved.

IT WAS ONE of those shit-hot July afternoons when the birds fly around with their mouths open, and I found Beezer sitting on his ass at the end of his dirt driveway, like he had just fallen from the heavens and didn't have a clue where he was. When I saw Flynn's matte-gray VW parked up by the house, I knew Beezer was whacked on something stronger than Coors. Flynn was always figuring some way to get high: harvesting peyote buttons, boiling out the opium tar from highway poppies, smoking the dried insides of banana peels.

Like Beezer, Flynn had too much time on his hands, but unlike Beezer, he didn't have a house, so he was always sponging off someone.

"Beezer, buddy," I said, "what's your problem?" I got out of my truck and nudged him on the shoulder.

He just swayed catatonically and grinned. He wasn't wearing his sunglasses, and his one good eye was dilated black like a hockey puck, even out there in the afternoon's white light. The fresh, pink sun damage was practically throbbing off his face, and I knew I had to take him inside.

"Get up, man," I said. "What'd Flynn give you?"

No answer, so I hefted him to the house and plopped him on the couch. Flynn was in there, his skinny, half-naked body curled into a pale, twitching ball under the kitchen table. Flynn, I didn't give a shit about. There were no pipes, no funny smells, no needles, nothing to indicate how they had gotten wasted.

"Close your eyes, Beezer," I said. "I'll get you some water." I was used to it, but every time Beezer got fucked up, especially when Flynn was involved, it scared me.

MY BROTHER BRIAN would come home trashed like that all the time when I was a kid. He'd stumble into my room, laughing or coughing or just looking around at all my toys and books with big, amazed eyes. He was seven years older, and the first few times he chose to sober up in my room, I was scared, thinking that when I got into junior high and high school, I'd have to get wasted, too; thinking that it was part of it all, required.

My parents were no help. They blossomed socially in their late thirties, around when Brian started ninth grade. My father sported a tight perm and a three-inch-wide watchband. My mother's hair was feathered, and her overtanned skin was like canned gravy. They were part of the Tucson Racquet Club scene: new prefab homes in the foothills, racy parties with swinging couples and cocaine, roller disco at Skate Country, chiropractors. They were cool, and they wallowed in it all. They mellowed after Brian died. My father read more, and my mother let her skin heal.

Caring for my brother was almost a nightly ritual—I knew to get him water and how to keep him quiet. I was good at it until near the end. About a week before he died, I awoke at two or three in the morning with his tongue squirming around in my mouth, warm and fatty feeling, and his sparse whiskers scraping my chin and nose. As it was happening, I was dreaming there was a wild animal in my mouth that I couldn't spit out. I finally woke up because I was suffocating. I shoved him off with my arms and legs, and he hit the floor.

"My own brother," Brian said, crying, squatting next to my bed. "My own brother kissing me like that."

"I didn't," I said.

"For a six-year-old, you're a fucking pervert."

"I'm ten, and I didn't do anything."

He wasn't listening. He stood up and staggered over to my fish tank. He flicked on the purple light and stared in. He was glowing, casting jittery shadows all over my room.

"Want water?" I asked him. "I'll get you water." I sat up and wiped my mouth on my pajama sleeve.

"You did it," he said. "Not me. You Frenched me."

"I was asleep. How could I?"

"You're really fucked in the head." He flicked off the tank light and lumbered down the hall.

I went into the bathroom and brushed my teeth until the toothpaste foam plopping from my mouth was pink with blood. I worried that night, nauseated, my mind racing. Had I kissed him first? I was asleep, I reasoned, I couldn't have.

The coyotes, they kept me awake for hours with their distressed, squealing frenzy of yips—even with my window closed and my pillow wrapped around my head. Police sirens would get the coyotes rolling. Sometimes I couldn't distinguish between sirens and coyotes, they'd mix, and I'd feel the noise in my stomach with another spurt of adrenaline each time the pitch got higher.

When my parents went to Vegas that next week, more than twenty of Brian's wasted friends invaded the house. They all looked older than Brian, the guys with thick, muttonchop sideburns they could chew on; the ladies, big-hipped, clog-wearing types, shimmying around the place in their cutoffs and halter tops. They had a hookah bubbling in the living room, five of them sucking hash through snaky tubes, sitting on my mother's Oriental rug. There was a keg out back near the pool in a Rubbermaid trash can full of ice. I remember my dad emptying that keg into the bushes a few weeks later; the rancid, yeasty stench crept all the way up to my room on the other end of the house.

I tried to watch things at the party, but there were too many people to keep track of, so I ended up only following Brian, who was capering around, indulging in a little bit of everything, adjusting his stereo until Robert Plant's high, dangerous voice was just right: *You need coolin'. Baby I'm not foolin'.*

I tried to be stealthy, but Brian noticed me on the stairs above the family room as he painted a rocker chick's belly with my poster paints. The chick was sprawled across the coffee table, her head dangling off the end, Styx baseball shirt hiked up to her breasts, and lace-up jeans untied a little. He smeared all the colors together into rude shades of green and brown, fingering in swirls and making a flower around her navel. When he spotted me up there, he yelled, "Want something, pervert?" and flicked his tongue at me like Gene Simmons. The rocker chick laughed, and sat up, spilling the paint into her jeans.

I knew jumping into the pool from the roof was risky, but I didn't protest. I just watched it all from the kitchen window, pressing my face against the screen, hearing the thuds from their footsteps above me. Some guys were doing flips or cannonballs, barely missing the side of the pool. The girls were in the water cheering them on, naked, with their white breasts floating in front of them.

Brian tripped up there, and when I heard the dull thunk of his head on the cement deck below, I knew he was dead. He had peeled away most of his back on the way down, scraping it on the red Mexican roof tiles. Someone rolled him over as I got out there, and Brian's dazed face looked toward the Catalina Mountains.

They all stood around, dripping, naked, dumbfounded, some of the girls screaming, turning away, stomping their feet in distress. One guy leaned over and blew in Brian's mouth. Dark blood drained from his ear.

WITH BEEZER MOANING on the couch and Flynn still quivering under the table, Becky pulled up in her brown Toyota. I was thinking she was there to take me back, to deliver me from my responsibilities with Beezer. I almost went in the other room to gather my stuff, but she was quick to the door, running up the path from the driveway.

Staring at drugged Beezer but talking to me, she said, "I brought this. I know how much it means to you." She pulled my hat out of her knapsack and tossed it at me. "It was on top of the fridge. I just kept forgetting about it." She had gotten her hair cut, not much, but she looked younger, neater.

"Thanks."

"I finished my dissertation—for real this time. It's been officially submitted."

"Congratulations," I said, thinking she was probably both sad and psyched that she never had to look at Botero's distorted fat people again. "A lot happens in a week."

"Fun afternoon at Beezer's?"

"No," I said. "It's not that fun."

She turned on her way out and said, "By the way, your truck's at the end of the driveway. The door's still open and the radio's on, tuned to a hick station."

It clouded up black that afternoon. The doors stuck with humidity, and the swamp cooler offered no relief. All I could do for Beezer was aim an electric fan at him and pat his forehead with a wet washcloth. I even wiped Flynn's forehead a few times.

When Beezer woke up that night, his rolled eye was back to normal, looked fine, even when I closely examined it with a flashlight, watching his pupil constrict. "It feels a little funny," he said, thumbing it. "Like I just got a haircut or had a cast removed. It feels new."

We sat on an old pine bench on his front porch, staring out into the purple-dark desert, plugging down Coors and breathing in the creosote smell released by the quick monsoon that had plowed through the sky a few hours after Becky left. Beezer and Flynn had swallowed jimson seeds that morning, and Beezer said he had seen everything in two dimensions. I didn't know what it was like for Flynn, who was still sleeping under the kitchen table, but Beezer said it was cool. He had stopped at the end of his driveway and sat in the dirt because he thought he was going to bump into the mountains.

"They were right there in front of me, only they were waist-high," he said.

"Oh," I said, "you were like Godzilla."

"Mothra," he said. He kicked a crumbled can off the porch. "You know, Sam, we should hit Nogales on Friday. I can drive now that my eye's fixed. I'll find that donkey and kick his ass."

I ignored Beezer's stupid joke and tried to imagine everything in 2-D, people sliding around like paper dolls, houses and cacti flat, but still standing, all pressed together like a collage of cutout magazine photos. I couldn't get it right in my mind because legions of Botero's fatties—round, jiggling, about to explode with plumpness—they invaded my image and brought the third dimension with them. Then I gazed across the desert for the headlights from Becky's car, hoping she'd be pulling into the muddy driveway any minute but knowing she wouldn't.

I looked over at Beezer, who was still jabbering about the donkey in Nogales, and wondered why the hell he was out on his front porch getting drunk after a day like he had. Why was he so excited to get back down to that depressing strip club?

To see Beezer on a horse was an amazing thing. The horse—practically any horse—was an extension of him. On a horse, he didn't look dumb, he looked right, at ease, with no stupid grin. At the guest ranch where he used to work, people practically rallied around him. Tourists from New York or Boston in stiff new Wranglers would insist on Beezer being their teacher. So why was he out there on the porch, belching now and then, with seven or eight empty Coors cans scattered at his bare feet?

I STEPPED AWAY from Brian and sat on the diving board. I pulled my knees up to my chest and watched all his stoned friends try to deal with the situation. One commanding woman wearing an Aunt Jemima bandanna on her head kept warning everyone that she was about to call an ambulance, and *ambulance means cops.* They all scattered like ants, grabbing their shoes and bags, running around the pool area through dangerously slippery puddles. One fat guy, shirtless, with breasts resting on top of his woolly stomach, wasn't running like the rest. He looked around nervously—eyes moving like rubber balls—as he shot his cup full of beer from the keg. He chugged that beer, took a deep breath, and filled his cup again, all while people dashed by him, frantic like they were all about to be bombed. When the fat guy saw me looking at him, his shoulders dropped. He tossed his cup and moved like the rest. A few guys said they couldn't just leave Brian like that. One of them grabbed a giant beach towel with a pink flamingo emblazoned on it, and draped it over Brian so we could no longer see his dead eyes.

Those fucking sirens drove me crazy—ripping through my head—and then this insincere paramedic woman came over to me on the diving board and started blowing standard questions my way.

"Can you turn those sirens off?" I said to her. "Please." I watched over her meaty shoulder as a few other paramedics went to work on Brian. They covered his face with a plastic breathing device, looked at his eyes with a penlight, stuck a tube in his mouth. One guy said, "No way," and then they started loading Brian onto a stretcher—and all this time the paramedic lady was in my face, asking her dumb obvious shit: "There was a party here? . . . He fell from the roof? . . . He hit his head pretty hard?" She didn't do anything about the sirens, which got louder and faster.

Then instantly all the energy drained from me; my arms and legs felt like bags of dirt, and my eyelids were closing me off. I walked away from the woman, by about ten cops and paramedics all scribbling into little notepads, by our neighbor Mrs. Parsons, who told me she'd stay until my parents got back from Vegas, and on up to my room.

I thought it was Brian who woke me later, and I stood up about ready to get him water. It was either dusk or dawn; the dirty brown light was seeping through my curtains and filling my room. I had been sleeping for either one hour or twelve—I couldn't tell. When I determined the figure standing at my door wasn't Brian, I sat back down on my bed and switched on my lamp.

I knew who it was before my eyes completely adjusted— I saw the dried paint splotches on her jeans. Her hair was matted up on one side, and she was shoeless. "What the fuck?" she said blankly.

"What?" I said.

"Where is everyone?" She looked at her jeans and shirt like she was surprised to see they were smeared with colors. She raked her fingers through her hair, then shook her hand like she had touched something nasty. "I went downstairs and there was an old lady watching TV, but I can't find anyone else."

"That was Mrs. Parsons, I bet," I told her. "You didn't hear the sirens?"

She tottered over to my bed and sat down next to me, staring straight ahead at my fish tank. "Why does your brother call you a pervert?" she said, grinning drowsily. I could smell the dried puke in her hair—like Parmesan cheese.

"I don't know," I said.

She seemed disappointed. She had expected a good story, like Brian catching me masturbating with a dirty magazine or discovering me rifling through my mother's panties and bras. She wanted me to divulge a sickening secret. She sighed, then tried to blow her clumpy bangs out of her eyes. "When did the party get busted, anyway?"

"That's not really what happened," I told her.

prayers for beans

AS USUAL, HARPER stopped by Maxim's parents' house the night Maxim returned from graduate school for winter break. Harper carried the big clay pot of frijoles against her stomach, standing with her legs apart for support. Her hair was bunned, but Maxim noticed how a few loose frazzles blew in the easy desert breeze, played in the light spilling from the front door.

"You went three times?" Harper said, hugging the pot tighter. These frijoles—Maxim's reward—had always been perfect: runny and spicy, but not blow-your-head-off spicy, and just a suspicion of cilantro.

Maxim was aware that to Harper he was nothing but a means of communication with Saint Jude, an intermediary for the miraculous blessing. But he didn't care; he was used to it, and in return, he got the beans and the sickeningly pleasant rush in seeing her.

When she flashed her flirty-kitty half-smile at him, obviously holding back a real one, he forgot the dangerous drivers in Baltimore, forgot the gauntlet of belligerent street people he had to pass to enter the shrine. "Thrice," he said, staring at her mouth, waiting for her mild smile to expand. "Once in the beginning of the semester, and twice this month."

"And you prayed William would stay out of fights?"

"You ask me that every time," he said.

Harper's brother, William Watson III, loved fighting and women and drinking and crashing trucks—he always had. He was a grade below Maxim in prep school, and once, when Maxim was a senior and William was a junior, William brought a hooker to the prom. She was done up in a black vinyl dress and dangerously high heels. Her stockings were seamed fishnet. On the dance floor, the hooker grabbed William's ass, kneaded it, and pulled him in. With her bursting cleavage and mane of crimped yellow hair, he paraded her around like she was a Texas debutante, introduced her to the headmaster and the headmaster's frumpy wife. Maxim saved William—as was often the case back then—by arguing in William's defense at the disciplinary board meeting: "The prom invitation clearly states that guests from other schools are welcome. Miss Bassini is a pupil at the Arizona Academy of Beauty," he'd announced to the board. "Is our school so snobby, so elitist, that we refuse to recognize the Arizona Academy of Beauty as a school?"

Now he answered Harper: "I prayed that he'd stay out of trouble in general—like I always do."

She sighed. He invited her in, but she said, *"Tengo que salir.* Sorry," and she handed over the beans like she was suddenly anxious to get rid of them. Maxim lifted the lid and dipped his thumb in the mush like it was frosting. She glanced back at him from the walkway before she disappeared behind the dense, swaying oleanders.

Maxim watched from the dark dining room as she cruised off in her shiny Land-Rover. William, almost on cue, pulled his ratty truck into the billow of dust her car had kicked up.

Maxim was exhausted from exams and the six-hour flight. His eyes were heavy and stinging. He'd wanted to sit at the table and devour a plate of beans before heading off to bed, but William relentlessly laid on the horn, so beans and sleep were now impossible.

When Maxim jumped into the truck, William handed him a warm beer and said, "When do you finish with all this college shit, anyway?"

"Maybe sooner than I'd like," Maxim said, breathing in the reassuringly familiar smell from William's truck: fast food, spilled Jack Daniel's, chewing tobacco.

"Was that my sister's car pulling out?"

"No," Maxim lied. "That was my mom's friend."

"You know where Harper's working now?" William said. "At a tortilla factory. My dad almost shit when he found out."

"I wonder how many Ivy League grads make tortillas," Maxim said.

Harper had been speaking with an affected Mexican accent and wearing brightly embroidered dresses from the shops just across the border in Nogales since Maxim first met her years ago. They'd been in the same tennis clinic the summer before ninth grade, and they both ended up at Green Fields Country Day School that September. At first Harper asked people to call her Consuela Maria Martinez— all three names—but no one did. Lucy Gomez told Harper, "You're about as Mexican as Princess Diana." Harper had beautifully feral blond hair and more freckles than not.

It wasn't until senior year that Harper learned Maxim's middle name. After physics class one afternoon, she skipped over to where he was sprawled on a rickety picnic table. Maxim was quizzing William, who lay prone in the weeds under the table. "Copper," Maxim said through the planks of wood.

"C O?" William guessed.

"No," Maxim said. "C U. Like *see you* at the copper mine."

Harper busted right up to Maxim, ignoring her brother under the table. "Your middle name is Jude." She was barefoot, and Maxim noticed that the tops of her feet were tanned and freckled. She wore a shapeless turquoise peasant dress and carried the wooden flute she'd carved and meticulously painted in art class: tiny blue flowers, geckos, stars, planets.

"I know," Maxim said. "What's yours?"

"That's not what's important," she said, looking him over and nodding. *"San Judas Tadeo es el patrón de los casos desesperados."* Her mussed hair seemed reddish in the shade of the budding pomegranate trees.

"Okay," Maxim said. He sat up. The table creaked.

"You have a good middle name," Harper said.

"You have anorexic ankles," William told his sister from under the table.

But Maxim wasn't named after Saint Jude. His parents were Beatles fans. In those old pictures, they looked cool, relaxed: his father with moppy hair and dark purple glasses, his mother in a beret and a black turtleneck sweater. For years his mother had stored coupons in her tin *Yellow Submarine* lunchbox.

MAXIM AND WILLIAM sped through the night toward the airport, past track homes festooned with blinking Christmas lights, and past homely new southwestern-style strip malls painted in various shades of teal and pink. With the window rolled down, the dry, cool desert air felt right on Maxim's face—it felt nothing like Baltimore. He breathed it in and pepped up.

They skidded into the parking lot of the Golden Spur, a honky-tonk with a mechanical bull, a sawdusty floor, and real prostitutes who conducted their business in the attached motel rooms. Some nights chickens pecked at cigarette butts in the ashtrays on the bar and goats chewed on anything they could get. William was a Spur regular, even though he looked nothing like a cowboy: his hair was a floppy red tangle, and he only wore khakis and wrinkled oxford shirts. But he was one of the few people who had ever ridden the bull on level ten for more than eight seconds, and because of it, the prostitutes gave him special rates and knew his name. Maxim couldn't figure out why he was envious of William's Spur status—he found two-stepping foolish, and he was deathly afraid of the brazen prostitutes.

Misty and Icy toddled up to the truck as soon as William ground it into park. Misty tripped, and her big blond Dolly Parton wig slid off her head into the dirt. She stood up by herself—Icy didn't help her—and she shook the dust out of the wig, before placing it over her darker, clipped-up, natural hair. Icy, with her lazy left eye, sauntered up to the truck and smiled, exposing big wet gums.

"Hi, William and Friend of William," she said.

"Hi," Maxim yelled.

"You boys feeling lonely?" Misty said, adjusting her wig in William's side mirror.

William said, "Sorry, ladies," and started his truck. "I can't deal with this tonight." He put his truck back in gear and skidded out of the parking lot. "It's mean, I know," he said to Maxim.

"Yes," Maxim said. He slurped the last few metallic-tasting drops of his beer. "They seemed excited to see you."

"I've exhausted this town, Maxi Pad," he said. He steered his truck up a twisty ramp onto I-10, handing Maxim another warm Coors from the ripped box on the floor.

"You should go back to college and finish," Maxim said.

"I'd rather live in a cave."

A few nights earlier, sitting there in Baltimore at his crowded desk, Maxim had thought of Harper and the frijoles. The image had helped him plow through the countless equations and tedious reports. It had helped him forget all the professors who thought they'd made a big mistake by letting him into their program, how those professors would most likely ask him to leave in the spring with a consolation master's degree and not permit him to continue with his Ph.D. He had closed a fat thermodynamics book and gazed out his steamed window into the yellow-lit alley. Two rats were gnawing and tugging at what looked like a third rat. One hundred and twelve more hours, he'd thought, 112 more hours until Harper and the beans.

He and William zoomed past the Speedway Boulevard exit, the one for Grant, then the exit for Orange Grove Road. Every morning on his way to school, half-asleep, Maxim had driven on Orange Grove. He used to imagine what the land had looked like when there were no malls or spray-painted convenience stores, only rows of orange trees and small horse ranches.

IT WAS MID-APRIL and their college acceptance letters had arrived. In the mornings, the seniors capered around for a while, skipped calculus class, sat on the crumbling adobe wall near the goats' pen, and gossiped about sex. Every part of campus—even the chemistry lab—held the dense, tart aroma of citrus and cactus blossoms, and everyone looked healthy in the perfect eighty-degree breezes. Water wars would break out around lunchtime: sloshing buckets, drenched T-shirts, water balloons, squeals, and usually a finalizing shove into the pool. By eighth period, they'd all stretch out on the rich, moist lawn in front of Baltzell Memorial Hall, stoned on sneaked Mexican ditch weed, and stupid because they didn't have to be smart anymore. They'd let the beating yellow sun work its ways, dry their clothes, darken their skin.

Harper was everyone's focus. She'd been accepted to Yale, where she'd study Spanish. "Mexican Spanish. If they try to shove that elitist Castilian *caca* at me, I'll leave." The untroubled seniors, Maxim included, followed her around like she had all the answers. But she didn't seem to notice. She went about her usual jaunty flute-blowing and dress-twirling and spent hours glazing hundreds of ceramic beads, which she eventually sold at a street fair to raise money for Nicaraguan refugees.

Maxim had been finding Saint Jude prayer cards all over school that spring: in books and magazines in the library, taped above drinking fountains, stuffed into the return change slot of the Coke machine. Each card held the image of Saint Jude, rendered in muted blues and greens, clutching a giant coin to his chest with one hand, gripping his wooden staff with the other. Then there was that odd puff of hair in the middle of his head—like a dying gray flame.

Someone glued a card above a urinal with chewing gum. No one defaced the card, but scrawled next to it was HARPER = PSYCHO POSEUR MEXI-CHICK. Maxim spat on the graffiti and thumbed it away.

He'd read the cards often, sometimes unwittingly, and he came to incessantly recite the prayer in his head: *Saint Jude, faithful servant and friend of Jesus, the Church honors and invokes you universally, as the patron of hopeless cases.* . . . The teachers looked at him in class like he was high, but most of the time it was the unsummoned prayer squirming through his mind that triggered his daze.

A few weeks before prep school commencement, Harper caught Maxim reading a card as he waited to use the pay phone. She strolled up and said, "It works. How do you think I got into Yale?"

"You're smart, and your dad went there?"

"Your middle name," she said, scratching her ankle with her flute. "You're forever connected—blessed." She stopped scratching and looked at Maxim like he was a big white light.

"Okay," he said.

She blinked hard. "You want to come to dinner tonight?" she asked. "At my friends' place?"

"Sure," Maxim said, "I guess."

Harper took Maxim's hand and jotted an address on his moist palm: *62 West Simpson.* The pen tickled. "It's a party, so you can bring whomever." She skipped off but turned around. "Don't bring William. He doesn't understand my friends."

Maxim didn't bring anyone. He drove the narrow brick streets of Barrio Viejo in the shadow of Sentinel Peak, feeling boxed by the closely fitted ancient adobe homes, pretending he was in a different country, somewhere exotic and a little dangerous, like Brazil or Honduras. He parked on the end of Simpson and ambled along the dusty, tiled sidewalk until he found number sixty-two.

Maxim peered through a large window and saw Harper

dancing. She was smiling broadly, really grooving, hitching her skirt and pumping her hips. Her man, with his slick, pomaded hair and killer white teeth, moved like a pro, like an extension of Harper. The fast and trumpet-heavy *norteño* record was tormentingly audible from outside. When Maxim placed his hand on the window, he felt the vibrations. He jogged back to his car.

TWO HOURS LATER, William turned onto Indian School Road. "Gas," he said. "We're in Phoenix."

"Why?" Maxim mumbled from half slumber. It was three A.M. Baltimore time, and he hadn't gotten much sleep because of his exams. He'd finished one only fourteen hours earlier, right before he caught the train to BWI airport.

The beer was drained. The empties clanked around on the floor, trying to tease Maxim. But Maxim didn't want more beer. He wanted only to be asleep in his childhood bed at his parents' house, knowing that when he woke up, there would be plenty of food to choose from in the kitchen. He imagined breakfast: scrambled eggs, steaming flour tortillas, electric green poblano salsa, and a small delectable swamp of Harper's frijoles. In Baltimore he often ate cereal for all three meals.

William didn't turn back toward I-10 after he pumped the gas; he drove the opposite way, into the prefab sprawl of Phoenix, under a million street lamps, past shopping centers, all of them lighted up like football games even though it was midnight.

"We played soccer down here once," William said. "At that school near the red mountain. Remember that school?"

"Vaguely," Maxim said. "That was six or seven years ago."

His mouth was pasty. To his tongue, his teeth felt furry. He wanted his toothbrush.

Maxim fell asleep, his head pressed against the cool window.

BACK WHEN MAXIM had been an undergraduate in North Carolina, Harper called him. "William told me that you're going to graduate school in either Baltimore or Chicago," she'd blurted, neglecting to identify herself.

Maxim knew it was Harper even though this was the first time they'd spoken since scattering to different colleges almost four years earlier. He'd almost forgotten to care about her. "I might," he said.

"Don't you think it's a little too mystical?" she asked. "I mean with your middle name and all?"

"I don't get it."

"The Saint Jude shrines!" she screamed into the phone. "There's one in Chicago and one in Baltimore. The one in Chicago is the *official* national one, but the Baltimore one is supposed to be more powerful."

"I'm not familiar with shrines, Harper."

"Saint Jude. Shrines of Saint Jude."

"Sorry," he said.

"On the back of the prayer cards the addresses for the shrines are listed," she said. "On the bluish ones, it says Chicago; on the brownish ones, it says Baltimore."

"I remember the bluish ones," Maxim said. The prayer worked its way into his head again. He knew it better than the concepts and equations related to molar enthalpy, the subject of the worksheet on his desk. "What are you doing after graduation?" he asked her.

"Moving back to the barrio to teach in a bilingual kinder-garten," she said. "I hope."

Back to the barrio, Maxim thought. Her father's house was nowhere near the barrio; it was perched on a canyon wall in the foothills of the Santa Catalina Mountains. A peanut-shaped pool, tennis court, hypergroomed Xeriscaping.

"I'll mail you something," she said.

A few weeks later, a UPS guy placed a heavy box the size of a TV at Maxim's door in the dorm. Inside, swaddled in bubble wrap, was a ceramic Saint Jude lawn statue: green robe, giant coin, and the puff of hair. On the underside: HECHO EN MEXICO. Tucked snugly next to the statue were four votive candles, each with a painted image of the saint. A note, too: *Jude, I'll contact you in Chicago or Baltimore regarding pilgrimages to the shrines.—Harper.* Being addressed as Jude was weird, wrong.

He set the statue by the deep freezer in the lab where he worked on his senior project. Saint Jude stood proudly, watching over the young scientists. Everyone got a kick out of him. Someone made a hat for him out of a Coke can.

WILLIAM THREW THE empty beer cans at Maxim to wake him up. They thunked Maxim's head. "Be awake," William said. "I need you to drive."

"What?" Maxim said. "Leave me alone." And then Maxim was glad that he was no longer sleeping. He'd been dreaming that Doctor Head, his evil bastard thesis adviser, was yelling at him for screwing up the titration again. "What?"

"Let me get set, and then I need you to lay on the gas," William said. He was dripping wet, smelling faintly of sewage, standing by the open driver-side door.

"What the hell?" Maxim said.

They were parked on a dirt road next to a cement canal as wide as a basketball court. Maxim could hear the canal water moving swiftly, see the ripples catching the yellow shine from the moon. Behind William, bathed in flood-lights, was a family's backyard: wicker furniture, lime green sod, and a patch of prickly pear cacti with pads as big as fry-ing pans. A small-sounding dog barked nervously from a few yards over. Maxim felt the dog's high-pitched yips deep in his gut. And towering above everything was Camelback Mountain. Its gnarled peak reached into the velvet sky like an animal. "What are you doing? Why are you wet?"

"Water-skiing," William said. "Check this out." He pulled out a wad of shiny fabric from the bed of the truck. He stepped back, held two corners, and snapped it like he was setting a tablecloth. A flag: PHOENIX COUNTRY DAY SCHOOL EAGLES. "The rope from the flagpole's my towline. You just have to gas it when I say." He sloppily wadded up the flag and threw it at Maxim in the cab.

"You'll drown," Maxim said. "Or get hepatitis."

"Shut up."

"What're you using for skis?"

"It's more like a sled," William said. "A big plastic garbage-can lid. I got it from behind the cafeteria."

"You stole it," Maxim said, "like the flag and rope." Maxim knuckled the crusties from his burning eyes, thought about sleep. "Let's just go back to Tucson."

"Killjoy," William said, grinning madly, rocking from foot to foot like he was cold or excited. "This is perfect." He showed Maxim the garbage lid, how he'd tied the rope to the handle with double knots. "Just let me get back in the water, and you haul ass in the truck. I'll be sledding against the current."

"How will I know when to stop?" Maxim said. "How will I know how fast to go? I don't want to drag you to death."

"Don't blow a clot, man," William said. "Just listen for 'go,' and floor it. I want to go as fast as possible." He walked around the back of the truck holding the garbage lid like a huge shield.

Maxim adjusted the rearview mirror, but no matter how he tilted it, it wouldn't afford him a decent view of William in the canal. He hung his head out the window and waited for the word. The breeze was warmer and swampy-smelling. Camelback Mountain looked bigger, alive, like it might pounce on the whole scene. He heard William's splashes above the muffled rumble of the idling engine, watched the white rope lose slack, straighten, but he couldn't see William in the black sparkling water. Was he tangled up in the rope? Floating away, pale and bloated, to Apache Junction or to wherever the canal flowed?

Finally Maxim heard the command echo off the sides of the canal: "Gas it, Max! Gas the hell out of it!"

IT HAD BEEN a heavy and humid ninety degrees when Maxim first arrived in Baltimore for graduate school. Walking through the pressing, draining heat had been torture, so he signed a lease on the third apartment he saw. The rental office was generously air-conditioned, and the manager, a perky pregnant woman, seemed honest. It wasn't until after he signed the lease and paid the deposit that he noticed the Dumpster right outside his window. The apartment wasn't air-conditioned, and when he put a fan in the window, it blew in the stench of carrion and brown lettuce from the trash.

Maxim received a registered letter from Harper the second week he was there:

Jude, The shrine's on Polk Street, two or three miles from your place. Please go and light a candle for William. My father thinks he's high on pills and booze. He still won't go back to college, and he had a black eye the other day.

But it was too hot to ride his bike anywhere, too hot and way too humid to do anything but sit in his apartment with a wet towel on his face and listen to unfamiliar radio stations. He barely staggered to classes.

Maxim didn't visit the shrine until Harper called him three weeks later. "Sorry," he told her, "been too busy." He'd wanted to make a clean break from Harper and forget the prayer. He was sick of it clogging his brain.

She knew he was lying. "You've been there over a month. If you're really William's friend, you'll go down there."

He was trapped. He knew he couldn't lie about going to the Saint Jude shrine, he might anger God or Saint Jude—or both!—although he wasn't sure why. "I will."

"What do you miss about Tucson?" she asked him.

"People who know how to deal with the heat, and Sanchez bean burritos," he said, even though he was thinking that he missed her smile and riding around in her brother's truck.

"I make frijoles," she said. "Authentic ones. I learned from a woman in Hermosillo. You pray for William at the shrine, and I'll make a pot for you when you get back to Tucson."

"You don't have to," he said. "I promise, I'll go down there."

She sighed. "Go three times before Christmas. I'll make you beans." She hung up.

He traced the route on his map of Baltimore with dental floss: four point six miles. He dug his helmet out of the closet.

. . .

MAXIM FLICKED ON the parking lights and floored the loose-feeling pedal. The tires spun in the dirt a few seconds before he felt them catch, and he was pushed back into the smelly, threadbare seat.

His eyes darted from the dirt road to the rearview to the speedometer. The wind in the truck made Maxim's eyes water. The fast-food wrappers swirled around like little ghosts. Thirty, thirty-five, forty, forty-five . . . Maxim heard William's rollicking whoops and felt proud to be a part of the stunt, important and comfortable speeding through the night alongside the canal behind this sleeping neighborhood. But what would Harper think? A flash of guilt ignited his gut as he remembered the prayers he'd said and the beans he'd received over the last few semesters.

When the Phoenix Country Day School flag flapped up off the seat and draped itself over Maxim's face, he mistook it for an animal—some beast had flown into the truck and was attacking him, smothering him. He stomped the brake and the truck fishtailed dangerously close to the edge of the water, finally sweeping the opposite way into a pile of yard waste. Before he was able to pull the flag off his face and wave away the dust, Maxim heard William yell, "Hey!"

IT WAS A MISTY October day the first time Maxim pedaled down North Charles Street on his way to light a candle. As he crossed 28th Street, obeying the traffic light, a man in a wide American sedan yelled, "You're not a car!" and threw a box of Chinese takeout at him. The soy sauce stung his eyes and sent him swerving into a stinky, water-logged couch someone had set out on the sidewalk.

The shrine sat on Polk Street in a forgotten section of Baltimore where crazy pantless crack ladies pushed shopping carts down the sooty sidewalks, and guys in pimpy leather hats who looked like they were extras on *Baretta* or *Starsky and Hutch* hung out like they hadn't moved since 1977. The streets were cobblestone and slick, so Maxim had to push his bike for the last few blocks. The peeling billboard in front announced THE SHRINE OF SAINT JUDE: WHERE MIRACLES HAPPEN.

From the outside, the shrine seemed more like a scam than a holy site. But when he entered, Maxim saw it was home to a parish with solemn women praying the rosary, posters for bake sales tacked up in the vestibule, and uniformed kids from Catholic schools lined up single file to confess their sins.

The votive candle that Maxim lit cost a dollar—folded into fourths and crammed through a small slot in an ancient tin box.

Even though Maxim had been raised without religion—his mother was a nonpracticing Jew; his father was a defensive atheist—he worried a little about praying to Saint Jude. He'd prayed to God before, he did it often as a child. Back then Maxim figured it couldn't hurt. At twenty-four he still thought it couldn't hurt. But he feared that praying to Saint Jude might annoy God, wondered why Saint Jude wasn't considered a false idol. He prayed anyway; he'd promised Harper he would: *If William Watson is a hopeless case, help him not be. . . .*

The hundreds of flickering votive candles caused the air to smell holy and substantial, and the slight buoyant purling sound they made recalled to Maxim the flute Harper used to play back at Green Fields.

LATER THEY SAT on the hood of William's truck, William wrapped up in the flag, both of them eating sweaty microwaved burritos from 7-Eleven. While trying to find their way back to I-10, back to Tucson, they'd stopped and pulled over where 40th Street ended at the runways of Skyharbor airport.

The crosshatched abrasions on the side of William's face were already puffing pink, flaring with infection.

"That canal was squirming with bacteria," Maxim said.

"It was worth it," William said, gingerly dabbing his face with a paper napkin. "Tell me again how fast I was going."

"Forty-five," Maxim said. "Maybe a little faster."

The sun swelled on the horizon, smearing the sky from liquid purple to filthy brown. They watched the jumbo jets float in from the east, slow down in the air, and land. Like cartoons, Maxim thought. They seemed fake, too close and giant and sluggish to be real. But their booming, ripping noise made them real.

Maxim and William graded the landings. One jet bounced four times, testing its hissing shock absorbers. Its red wing lights traced squiggles in Maxim's tired eyes. They gave it a D minus. Maxim imagined a ruddy-faced stewardess cursing the clumsy pilot under her minty-fresh breath.

"We found two good things in Phoenix," William said. "The sledding canal and this place."

"You can watch the planes in Tucson, too," Maxim said matter-of-factly.

One was drifting in, shredding the sky. "Not this close, you can't," William yelled. "And they're jets, not planes."

Maxim felt the vibrations on the hood. They jittered up into his stomach and head. They made his inner ears itch and tingle. The prayer kicked in: *Most holy apostle, Saint Jude . . .*

He glanced at William's injured face, then looked down at his feet, his wet, mucky sneakers. "I pray for you," he yelled. "I light candles for you at the Saint Jude shrine in Baltimore, and Harper makes me frijoles." The jet landed smoothly, squealed to a halt without bouncing. "I've been doing it for three semesters." Telling William felt good, like finally going to sleep after a long day.

"She never makes beans for me," William said. "Not even for my dad—and he loves frijoles." William swiveled on his butt and jumped off the hood. "I give that landing an A minus. Let's go."

Maxim tossed his unfinished burrito in the dirt.

And I-10 was clogged with drones in bubbly Asian sedans headed to cubicle jobs, and minivans full of holiday shoppers en route to Metrocenter or the outlets in Casa Grande. Maxim listened to William whistle along to a happy-go-lucky country song: *Did some honky-tonk healin' to get me over you . . .* He watched him bob his battered head to the twangs and not even react to the stop-start, slow-as-hell traffic. William didn't flinch or curse when a hotshot talking on a cell phone in a glossy convertible abruptly cut into their lane; he only braked gently and kept whistling.

Maxim had twenty-one days before he had to be back at school, bumbling around the lab. Twenty-one days of eating beans and wondering if he was praying for the right person.

s₁k₉a₈ ₆b o y,

JUSTIN GOT PUNCHED UP the other night. A hillbilly skin-head from Apache Junction nailed him in the parking lot of the Fine Line. Justin's whole face is puffy, and he has black stitches on his chin. He denies being beaten up; he claims he hit an oil slick on Via Entrada and his Vespa slid into the desert. That's dumb because lots of people saw the fight, and there's not a single scratch on Justin's scooter. The mirrors are all there, and the chrome wheel covers are still so glossy, they look liquid.

Justin will lie like that, and I'll nod through it, not ques-tion it.

"When do you get your stitches out?" I ask him after alge-bra. The hall is clogged with zombies pushing to the gym for a basketball pep rally.

Justin unzips his army parka but leaves it on as he digs

through his messy locker: books and old lunches, and CDs and tapes with cracked cases. "Looky," he says, pointing to his top shelf.

Two kinds: Bumble Bees and Christmas Trees. Bumble Bees are better. Pull the black and yellow tablet apart, and it's already powder inside. When you pull the Christmas Trees apart: tiny colored balls. You eat Christmas Trees unless you want to smash the balls. "That's a lot," I say. It's a bag the size of a fist.

"All set, Teddy," he says. "Set for a while."

JUSTIN HAS A milk crate full of crackly Jamaican 45's from the '60s: Desmond Dekker, the Maytals, the Skatallites, the Melodians, the Paragons, Alton and the Flames, Girl Satchmo . . . He bought them from a desperate skinhead whose Aryan wife had twins. This skin was dumb enough to get SKINHEAD tattooed on his forehead, so he had to grow bangs and gel them down to get a job. He sold the box of records to Justin for fifty bucks. The Girl Satchmo single alone is worth fifty.

I have all the same songs on CDs, but they sound too clean and inauthentic. We play the 45's on Justin's parents' old wood-paneled stereo console in their garage and skank around like chickens, just the two of us, each in our own trance. The music—the shit-hot, rock-steady blue beat—works its way into you and gives you those jumpy, eager waves in your stomach and electrifies your legs.

One time his dad caught us dancing to Derrick Morgan's "Festival Ten," jacking up our monkey boots like we were running through the tires in PE. *Ooh yeahhhh, rubba dubba dum dum dum . . .* Later his dad asked him if we were gay together.

MY BROTHER LANE sits on the front steps in the white draining afternoon sun. He's eight, and I'm supposed to be home at three so he doesn't have to wait too long. My dad won't let him be in the house by himself because last year he tried to make scrambled eggs and set his sleeve on fire. He still has the pink wrinkled scar on his forearm.

I swallowed two Christmas Trees before art class a few hours ago. That's all Justin would surrender. I couldn't hold the wet clay. It kept sliding off the wheel and slapping on the floor like a dying fish. Sitting there in front of the spinning wheel was difficult for me; my legs were twitching, moving to no music at all, my heart pumping hard against my ribs.

"You're late," Lane says. "As usual."

"Barely ten minutes." I burp, and it tastes like chalk.

On the steps, framed by the bleached stucco archway, Lane looks like a picture taken with cheap film. The blue and red stripes of his T-shirt are too bright, his face and messed blond hair are washed away in the glare. He's tossing his hacky sack in the air and catching it. I know guys who can stand around and keep the hacky going for hours, only using their feet. Lane is not one of them.

Next Tuesday it will be six years since I walked into the house and found Lane sitting on top of our mother, drawing on her face with her lipstick. March 16, 1980. Lane had eaten some of the lipstick, his own face was smeared with it, chunks of it stuck in his stupid grin, coating his baby teeth. Cans and carrots and cereal boxes were scattered across the Mexican tiles along with my mother's purse and keys. Her eyes were open but empty. Lane straddled her chest and bounced and clapped like he was riding a toy horse.

I yelled at Lane, and his face bunched up and he started

bawling and toddled into the family room. When I kneeled down next to my mom, I smelled the baby powder she used to sprinkle on after her bath, noticed how the air-conditioning vent was making a few loose strands of her blond hair fly up. I wiped the thick drool from the side of her face with my hand and tried to smudge away the lipstick mess. I called 911, but I could tell by the coldness of her skin that it was way too late.

I wrung a washcloth under the hot tap, the water burning my hands. I was going to clean her up before the paramedics got there. Lane peeked in, carrying one of my mother's sandals, holding it out toward me. He had stopped crying, but his fat cheeks were wet with tears and his nose was running—his whole face shined. "Do," he said, and I threw the hot cloth at him. It slapped the wall above his head, stuck for a second, and fell to the floor. Lane retreated into the family room, crying harder, gasping, because I scared him with the washcloth—not because our mother was on the floor with a burst artery in her head.

Lane still looks like he did six years ago—he never lost that chubbiness in his face, and he walks dink-toed, like he's wearing a dirty diaper. "I could have been abducted waiting here all this time," he says. "I'm telling."

"Go ahead and tell," I say to him. "I don't care." Lane will forget about my being late as he rots in front of afternoon talk shows and eats cereal by the handful.

Justin and I are going to a party tonight. Scooterists from Phoenix are rallying down. Linny and other mod chicks will be there, and they'll play old Motown and Stax, and we'll get drunk on Guinness and dance to Rufus Thomas and the Staple Singers.

"Open the door," Lane says. "I have to pee."

"Just pee in the oleanders." I hold the keys above him, make him jump.

"Open the door!"

"Jump."

"Fucker," he says.

I snatch his hacky and throw it over the wall into the pool.

"Open the door!" He's pinching his dick through his shorts and dancing around, rocking from one foot to the other.

IF I SHUT my blinds and tack a blanket over the window in my room, I can make it as black as night. I have hundreds of glow-in-the-dark stars stuck on my ceiling, and I'll lie there with loud music washing over me, and stare at them. I'll grip my bedspread, clenching the fabric until my forearms ache, and pretend like I'm being rocketed up there or that the stars are shooting toward me and I have to dodge them. Today, with the two Christmas Trees still working me, it almost feels real, almost seems like the glowing stars are shooting closer, like my bed is speeding through space. I turn up my stereo with my foot: *I lost a lifetime thinking of it. I lost an era day-dreaming like I do . . .* It's the wrong music, the Jam, and if Justin knew I listened to it, he'd get self-righteous and lecture me. Ska and pre-'76 soul only. But for now, this song is perfect, seems so alive as it weasels its way through my head.

When my dad opens the door later, the bright orange light from the hall spills in. The Christmas Trees have finished with me, and I'm lying in a puddle of my own energy. "Lane claims you were almost an hour late," he says. I roll over and squint at him. He's not wearing his glasses, and his eyes look small and sunken.

"That's a lie," I say. "I was like ten minutes late, and he called me a fucker."

"What're you doing in here, anyway?"

"Sleeping."

"You're all red," he says. He sits on my bed and puts his hand on my forehead. He runs his fingers through my flat-top. I smell the sweet whiskey on his breath. "You're all sweaty, too." He stopped at the Lunt Avenue Marble Club and had a few drinks today, probably tried to talk to a pretty woman who ignored him.

"Just tired."

"Where you going tonight?"

"A party," I say. "Scooterists from Phoenix are coming down."

"I don't want you on a scooter."

"No duh."

"I'm trying to have a normal conversation with you." My dad stands and pulls his khakis out of his butt. I hate seeing that. Makes him seem so old.

I PARK ON Ninth Street in front of the Buffet Bar, a few blocks from the party, but I can hear the music already. Otis Redding's "Respect" bounces off the candy-colored adobe houses, hits parked cars, then fizzles in the ten-foot bunches of prickly pear cacti. The song gets bigger, and I notice the shine of the Vespas and Lambrettas under the street lamp. The scooters are lined up, on display, and the scooterists are standing around in their knee-high Doc Martens and patch-covered bomber jackets, talking about engines and shocks and gears and paint jobs and rallies.

Justin's with them, showing off his own '65 Vespa 90 Super Sprint to a mod kid with sharp bangs and a turtle-neck. Justin nods at me, lifts his shades, and says, "Ted, go get yourself a beer and a woman." He grabs my hand. "And . . ." He dumps Bumble Bees into my palm like they're M&M's. His eyes are black disks, and his head's bobbing and twitching way too fast for the music. I bet he's lied to the mod kid about the stitches on his chin.

"You're jumpy, man," I tell him.

"Bumble Bees buzzing through my body," he says. "I'll be skanking all night." He grins so big, his stitches could pop.

"I'll get you a beer," I say, and I head into the music, into a booming flourish of tight trumpets and trombones.

Linny grabs my hand and drags me to dance with her. The room is packed, stinky with beer and savory spliff from the Rastas smoking up in the kitchen. A few rudeboys in suits and porkpies who I've never seen before are tossing cards at the wall, smoking, being cool. I pull Linny through the kitchen, grabbing a beer, and out the back door.

"Look," I say, holding out the Bumble Bees. They shine like plastic.

Light from the kitchen window makes her white lipstick glow, makes me want to kiss the glow. "I can't," she says. "I've got a meet tomorrow. I have to leave here at, like, eleven, so let's dance inside." She does a twirl in her go-go boots.

"You look totally good," I tell her. "Legitimate."

"You, too."

"Hold on," I say. I walk over to a rickety picnic table and open a few Bumble Bees onto the wood. I sniff it all and plug my nose. It burns through my head, but it kicks so fast, busts into me like nothing else. I feel it zigzagging down my body like a bunch of fire ants until my limbs fill with ticklish energy. Linny rubs my back and hands over my beer—opened for me, fumes twisting from the top.

"Now?" she says, looking toward the house, dancing a little.

"Hold on." I stand and kiss the glow, moving my mouth down behind her ear, nibbling where her hair stops on the back of her neck.

She stiffens, pushes me away some, and says, "Let's just dance."

"Okay," I say, stepping back. "Let me chug this." I sit down again and drink my beer, out of breath.

Linny stands there, one hand on her hip, smiling. "You're piggish," she says. "But you can dance." She's smart. She gets all A's at University High School. Plus she's the best in whatever swim event she does. But she doesn't have shoulders like most swimmers. She's decked every day, sometimes even wearing clip-on parts of fake hair— *wiglets,* she calls them—in crazy-ass '60s 'dos. I've never been to University High, but I bet her teachers respect her, and I bet the other students don't give her shit for being a mod like they would at my school. Sometimes, like now, I can't believe she's with me.

Soon Linny will fly away, escape this bullshit scene. I can tell. She'll be a mod professor or a mod scientist or a mod lawyer, and Justin and I will be roasting in Tucson, wishing we lived in a real city where you can see ska bands three nights a week.

But tonight the scene is good. Linny and I finally dance, to the sock-it-to-me rhythms of the Soul Children. The living room is crowded, everyone's looking sharp as shit, and everyone's dancing—but not like Linny and I, who have it down. For this song, we wing a mellowed watusi we learned from an old book Linny found at Thrift City. I can see Linny counting off the steps, whispering the numbers, lightly blowing them through her frosted lips.

The singer babbles about hearsay jive toward the end, and I keep repeating it at Linny, imitating his raspy voice: ". . . hearsay jive, baby. Hearsay jive, hearsay jive . . ."

"Shut up already," Linny says when the next record starts.

"Hearsay jive," I say, laughing. My stomach and ribs hurt.

"You're pathetic."

And one of the unfamiliar rudeboys walks over. "What's your problem?" he asks me. A few yellowed, sun-fried dreads poke out from under his hat. He's authentic, right down to the third button on his Carnaby suit, his flooded black trousers, and electric white socks. "You're fucking with the whole scene, dissing the Soul Children."

"Here," I say, and I flip him a Bumble Bee from my pocket.

He catches it, holds it up between his thumb and finger like a precious coin, and pops it in his mouth. "Got more?"

"No," I lie.

LINNY'S GONE. She disappeared without saying anything. Floated away, leaving me with all these people I don't really know and my heart leaping up, up, up, faster and faster.

The rudeboy's talking to me, telling me he and his buddies rode their scooters all the way from Anaheim, fourteen hours. They're going to the University of Arizona in the fall, and they're here to check out Tucson. "Is this the whole deal here?" he says.

I hear him and understand him, and I want to tell him sometimes good bands like Fishbone or the Untouchables come through, how we go to the veterans' building every other Saturday for reggae with the hippies, but I can't; I can only say, "Yup, yup."

My heart's pounding my stomach down, pushing my ribs out. It's like an animal, like a guinea pig or a rabbit or something squirming to escape from my chest. I have a cramp in my side, but I still want to dance, and I start skanking hard to the new Potato Five record that found its way onto the stereo. My body catches up to my heart, and the song helps me outrun the Bumble Bees. I close my eyes tight, and I can feel people moving away from me, giving me space to pick it up, thrash around—giving me my own bubble.

THE RASTAS ARE generous in their stoniness, and I think they got a kick out of watching me skank. They let me hit off their fat yellow bomber. It's tough to hold the smoke in my lungs with my heart racing, but I do it. I do it by thinking of something else, something vivid and emotional, as the smoke burns my lungs and my lungs burn for air. One of the Rastas can blow smoke out of one nostril at a time, long streams or little, quick puffs: left, right, left, left, right. "How?" I say to him, letting smoke sneak out between my teeth and past my lips. "How do you do that?" But he just smiles, his droopy pink eyes looking like there's nothing much behind them, like if they fell out onto the table, smoke would leak from the sockets like in a jack-o'-lantern. The Rasta on my right, a guy with four big dreads, each as wide as his arms and full of leaves and twigs, looks at me like I've outstayed my welcome, like he'd like to punch holes in my throat with the pearl-handled resin pick lying on the table next to a bag of choice buds.

I head out front to learn about scooters, but the pot hits me—makes my legs heavy and my skull feel open—and I squat down on the cement porch steps.

Justin's sitting on someone's red and white Lambretta. The mod kid's sitting on Justin's Vespa. They're both testing the shocks, banging their butts into the seats.

"No clearance," Justin says. "Like all Lambrettas."

And this wide, white American sedan comes screeching around the corner. Its horn plays "Dixie," and when it slows in front of the party, I see it's a carload of skinheads.

One hangs out of the car. He's got thick eyebrows and a

gun, a big heavy shotgun that strains his wrist. It's pointed at Justin, and I think, This is it. "Die, mod fags!" the skin yells, but he leans farther out of the car and aims the gun up at the stars before he pulls the trigger. A pop—not as loud as I thought it would be—and a ghost of smoke suspended there.

All the other skins are looking and laughing, their heads like volleyballs, hanging out of the car as it peels away. And Justin just sits there, and so does the mod kid, and I'm thinking, What if he had actually shot Justin? And I realize something mean, something bad. I might not be that bummed if Justin was blown to bits, knocked off the Lambretta onto his ass in a puddle of blood and chunks of himself. I would feel bad that he went through all that physical pain, and I would feel bad that he died. I would be sad for his mom and dad, and sad for his little sister, who thinks Justin's cool and brags about his scooter to anyone who'll listen. I would be sad for other people who missed him, but I wouldn't miss him. If he could disappear without being killed, I wouldn't be sad. And the whole time I'm thinking all this, Justin and the mod kid are acting macho, Justin saying he's going to kill the skinheads. "If I weren't so fucking wired, I'd be on their asses!" he says. "I know where half those fags live."

A bunch of people bust through the front door, run down the steps, and crowd Justin.

Linny slinks out, sits next to me on the porch steps. "What the hell happened?"

"I thought you left," I say. "I'm glad."

"They shot something?"

A few slow-motion Rastas slump by and stand below Linny and me on the steps. They smell like patchouli and dope and mumble about guns.

"The sky," I say.

"You look bad," she says. "You look pale."

"Need to mellow."

"I need to get going," she says, "I have to swim in seven hours." And she squeezes in my cheeks with two soft hands and makes my lips fish out. She gives me a quick kiss and says, "Wait a long time before you drive."

VESPAS LOOK PRETTY small, like they'd chug along at thirty tops, but Justin's been up to seventy on his. We're doing fifty on Campbell Avenue. I'm on the back of Justin's, and three other scooters are following us. The party broke up soon after the gunshot, and we're heading over to a skinhead named Tully's house. In front of everyone back at the party, Justin announced he's going to kick Tully's ass. He might be able to. I know Tully. I used to hang out with him back before he got into that white power scene. I told Justin that Tully probably wasn't even in the car, that he should leave him alone, and he said, "After all the Bumbles I gave you, you're being a total puss." Then he babbled about how they would never *really* use the gun and how most of the skins are still in junior high.

The scooterists who came with us look like pretty wimpy guys: thin, even in their bombers and parkas. The skinheads could beat them up easy. Maybe even Tully. At the stoplights, people in cars check us out: four Italian scooters, all glossy, all decked with custom paint jobs and mirrors. One of the Phoenix scooterists has fourteen rearview mirrors sprouting from the front of his Lambretta like peacock feathers.

As we speed up Campbell on the curvy roller-coaster part, the Santa Catalina Mountains are black and jagged against the purple sky. The cool March wind makes my eyes water, and the peaks wash and smear. When I blink, I feel cold tears swimming back toward my ears, and the mountains are sharp for a few seconds again. You can't do this in a car.

Tully lives in a place called Barrio Lego: eight cinder-block duplexes arranged like a compound around an empty spray-painted swimming pool that's jammed with skaters during the day. I used to hang there and watch the skaters riding the walls of the pool, spinning in the air, doing impossible flips and jumps, scabbing themselves up pretty good. Tully used to play Two Tone ska from an old sticker-covered boom box and sit on the edge with me. That's how I first got into ska. The music hitched itself to me immediately, and I'd go sit at the pool and wait for Tully to get home from work every afternoon when school was over. If I got there early enough, I'd help the skaters sweep the dust and leaves and cracked tiles out of the pool. Almost every day, Tully would expose me to a different ska band, first British ones like the Specials and Madness, and then older ones like the Upsetters and the Ethiopians. He knows more about ska than Justin ever will.

THE SCOOTERISTS CUT their engines at the end of the street so the skins in Barrio Lego don't hear.

"I drove, you push," Justin tells me.

I do, my legs burning, my lower back hurting. The street is paved, but loose gravel covers it, and the tread on my monkey boots isn't right. I slip a few times, almost let his Vespa fall. After the third near slip, he says, "You drop that, and I'll kick your ass after I kick Tully's."

"You push it."

"I drove."

"I didn't really want to come." I stop, nudge the stand down with my boot. I huff hard, leaning over, my hands on my thighs. I feel the Bumble Bees in my pocket.

"Puss." And he starts pushing it up. I hear his monkey

boots skidding, and I hope he trips and scrapes up his precious wheel covers and snaps off a few mirrors.

They go on, but I plop down on someone's dirt driveway and pull apart a Bumble Bee, probably wasting half of it. I sniff the powder right from the capsule halves. I lick my hands and wrists for any bitter powder I can taste, and lie back on the dirt and look at the moon, almost full, bright enough to leave its print on my eyes. A line of six or seven quail scuttle right by my feet, honking like squeeze toys.

I run up the hill to Justin and the rest. I'm energetic again. They're standing at the end of Tully's driveway. His ugly duplex is the one closest to the street. There are lights on inside.

"There could be, like, twenty skins in there," Justin says.

"I knew this was a waste of time," one of the scooterists says.

"I just need to know who's in there."

"This is bullshit," the scooterist says.

My toes are fisting and unfisting in my boots, so I say, "I will," and I run at the duplex, rip through the gravel before they can stop me.

The red curtains are drawn, but not tightly, and I can see a fat skinhead standing in the choppy radiance of the TV. His Levi's are down around his boots, and he's working his cock, beating off right there in the room with Tully and another skin who's also beating off. The other skin is lounging back in a big orange chair holding a beer with one hand and wanking with his other, lifting his hips some, squirming, pulling hard, kicking the empties near his feet on the floor. Tully isn't beating off; he's spread on the couch, watching the TV, without his shirt, eating Doritos from a bag, like nothing unusual is happening. You can count his ribs, and he has a thick black swastika tattooed on his pale, thin belly. When he was a ska skin, back when we were friends, Tully used to brag that he was going to go down to Mexico and get SKA'D FOR LIFE tattooed on his arm. He never did.

With my forehead pressed against the window, I can clearly hear the *oooh, oooh, fuck me, fuck me* and *waka waka* disco music from TV, and I feel my own dick filling up, finding its way through the slit of my boxers and rubbing against my pants as I hop around a little, as I watch them go at it in there.

A rock the size of a baseball thunks the wall next to the window. I turn around and see Justin chucking another rock right at me. It hits the glass before I can think. The window cascades into pieces, and dazzling triangles smash at my feet. A big "What the fuck!" from inside. Justin laughs, and they jump on their scooters before I can run back to them. One kick-start, another, another, and another. The engines sputter, chuggle, spray little streamers of white smoke. Justin waves at me, and they all zoom off, leaving me there at the end of the driveway with an aching hard-on, watching their red lights disappearing down the hill.

"I see you, Ted! I'll fucking kill you!" Tully calls from his front door. With the brightness behind him, he looks thinner, like a Martian.

"Justin did it!" I yell—not that it really matters. He already hates us both.

I run down the hill, really haul balls, cut left into the arroyo. The mesquite branches whip my face, but only sting for seconds. The big setting moon makes the sand look like snow, and I run through it—ankle deep—not even winded. Hop over the little ravine, run by the crumbling old stables. A clump of jumping cholla clings to my parka sleeve, but I don't stop to shake it off. At River Road, I enter the drainage tunnel, run my hand along the cement wall, close my eyes as I walk quickly through the sewer-stinky dark, hearing the cars rumble above me, concentrating hard: *no rattlesnakes, no murderers, no scorpions, no butt rapists . . .* When I'm out, I cut across the corner of the golf course, dodging the sprinkler, mucking up the green, my boots squishing through, feeling the suck of the moist ground.

I FLIP ON the pool light right after I climb over the stucco wall. The whole pool glows carnival-purple, and squiggly reflections jiggle up the side of the house. Lane's hacky sack is clumped with leaves at the bottom near the steps in the low end. I fish it out with the net and flick off the obnoxious light. I settle on the diving board, on my back, squeezing out Lane's hacky and looking at the stars.

Since the moon has sunk, the stars are thick, arranged in swirls, so dense it's scary. My dad used to lie on the diving board some nights. I saw him doing it a lot right after my mom died. Whenever I woke up to take a piss or get a drink of water, I could look out my window and see him, sprawled on his back like I am—even on cloudy nights, when there were no stars. His eyes were always open, and his arms were crossed over his chest like a mummy's. I've never asked him about it.

The diving board is cool, cold even, and the chill soaks through my pants and parka, freezes my ass. But I'm staying out here until the orange pushes through my eyelids and wakes me in the morning. Around that time, Linny will be diving off the starting block at the meet, swimming her way to another ribbon or trophy. I'd like to call her right now, hear her froggy-tired voice, tell her about tonight, what Justin did to me. But she needs to sleep so she can win tomorrow.

I sit up for a minute and unlace my monkey boots. I wiggle my toes and toss the boots over the wall into the desert, hear each one crunch into a dry bush. I know I'll go find them tomorrow, but right now I'm hoping I won't.

tilt-a-whirl

"THINK HE'S DEAF or a retard?" Freedah asked, pointing over Mary's shoulder with an empty glass.

Mary scanned the wood paneling, the yellowed rodeo photos, the dried crumbling dartboard; it all smeared and traced together—even the blinking beer neon—until she spotted him: a young man seated with two painted-up prostitutes at a corner table across the dusty barroom. He was grunting loudly. Mary focused on him, watched him animate his throaty, ursine noises with his elegant hands. His face was smooth and precise, like it had been produced with care. "Deaf," she said to Freedah. "And don't say 'retard.' "

"I doubt those hookers know sign language," Freedah said, leaning close enough so Mary could see the one snaggle tooth disobediently twisting from her smile. Freedah was still pretty, with her creamy skin and baby nose. When they went to the dog track on Thursday nights, Freedah always left with a few phone numbers crammed into the back pocket of her jeans.

"Maybe they know this sign," Freedah continued, as she rammed the index finger of her left hand through the *O* of the *OK* she made with her right hand.

Mary raised her own finger, signaling to the bartender that she wanted another round, the fourth: a seventy-five-cent draught and another shot of the tequila she knew was practically poison. It made her burps taste the way burning tires smell—ashy and toxic. But she didn't care. She imagined that her last shot had worked itself deep into the crinkles of her brain, rendering her dulled and content.

Mary again focused on the deaf man. His ball cap was turned backward so she could see his eyes—big with youth. He was younger than she had initially thought, maybe sixteen or seventeen, probably shaving once or twice a week. He danced way off beat with one of the prostitutes to a slow, maudlin country number—flapping his arms lightly and kicking up his boots. Mary thought the hooker should help him dance better. Then she said it aloud.

"He doesn't know," Freedah said, rubbernecking to watch the couple. "He looks happy, doesn't he?"

"No," Mary said. She tossed back the shot of tequila as soon as the bartender set it down, and sucked an already-sucked lime. As the prostitute pressed herself into the deaf boy, calming his movements, Mary waited for the bitter tang of rind to overpower the taste of the third-rate alcohol. The lime stung her cracked lips. She swallowed half of her new beer and wiped her mouth with the sleeve of her dungaree jacket. "If that boy was happy," she said, "he wouldn't be with those ten-dollar hookers."

"How's your boy?" Freedah asked.

"Chigger's more like a man now."

"Can't be more than thirteen or fourteen?"

"Just turned thirteen, but he's got more hair on his chest than Burt Reynolds," Mary said. "Bigger than a bull, too."

"Could be an extra Y chromosome. Buzz had that. That's why he was violent and sweat so . . ."

Freedah went on, but Mary thought of how Chigger had looked hateful and defeated that morning, barely catching her eyes with his own. He had applied a Band-Aid to his neck, and some of the wound it covered was leaking out around the adhesive—the infected brown of pus and thickening blood. When Mary asked him what had happened, he poured milk over his wheat flakes and said, "You did it to me with the nail-pulling end of the hammer last night, right after I called you a man-at-the-dog-track-screwing whore." He lifted the bowl to his nose, took a whiff, and dumped his cereal down the sink.

"You deserved it," she said. That morning she had remembered nothing of the altercation: no hammer, no man-at-the-dog-track-screwing-whore remark. "You'll be happy to know Clem won't be around here anymore."

"Monkey Lady," Chigger had called her.

"You better zip it, or I'll make another hole in your neck."

He flipped on the garbage disposal and mumbled something.

She might have actually done it. She'd lost a few hours before. Once, the morning after a party at Freedah's, she woke up in her car baking in the parking lot of a tire store just outside of Eloy. On the passenger seat was a pile of hair that she initially mistook for a wig. When she scratched her temple and felt nothing but a prickle, she realized it was her own black hair on the seat. She looked at herself in the rearview and saw someone who resembled her old gym teacher. She put her head on the steering wheel and cried. She never found the scissors.

Yesterday she and Roger, her buddy from the feed store, had killed the afternoon with a bottle of whiskey. Roger kept the whiskey behind boxes of outdated seeds in the sawdusty back room where they sold chicks and ducklings by the dozen. No customers, just slow time and the constant muffled chorus of peeps and honks. Mary and Roger emptied the bottle of whiskey before two, so Roger walked over to the liquor store and bought another. That was where Mary's memory of the day ended.

Now in the bar, as Freedah babbled more about Buzz's syndrome, Mary constructed the ugly domestic scenario in her mind: she had stumbled in, and Chigger had said those mean words. She had pulled her arm back to slap him, but he had caught her wrist and twisted. She grabbed the hammer with her other hand—it was always floating around the house, never where it was supposed to be when she needed it—and swung. It hit his soft neck, tugging at the flesh, ripping downward to the thick red hair that sprouted from under his T-shirt. Maybe she felt it graze the harder, ribbed windpipe. She could imagine Chigger's face contorting, like it did when he was a toddler spilling juice or bumping his head on the corner of the table, back when he'd bury his tears in her leg—the reason his father had first called him Chigger: "That boy never lets go." With a cinematic burst, blood gurgled from the hole. Chigger released her arm and touched the wound in disbelief, probing it with his finger, testing its depth. Mary ran to her bedroom and locked the door. What had she done with the hammer?

She'd finish up early tonight, mellow out after downing this last beer with Freedah. On her way home, she'd stop at the glowing twenty-four-hour supermarket and buy groceries for Chigger: eggs, bread, cereal, milk, juice—wholesome food items. She'd wake up before him for a change and have a tray of steaming scrambled eggs ready before he took off for school.

"I gotta pee," she whispered to Freedah, interrupting. When she stood, her latest shot of tequila imposed itself, challenging her balance more than she liked.

Tinny pop music and happy squeals poured into the rest room through a half-opened window. On her tiptoes, Mary looked out at the carnival across the busy street—that damn perpetual carnival in honor of nothing. The air was cool but stank of trash, so she closed the window and examined her reflection: lines cut through her face. Around her mouth, wrinkles ran perpendicular to her lips. No wonder Chigger calls me Monkey Lady, she thought. Mary the Monkey Lady. She promised herself that she'd apply sunscreen in the morning, every morning from now on. She'd stick a note to her vanity tonight.

There was a new round of drinks on the table when Mary returned, and for a second she thought she hadn't drunk her last ones. "My treat," Freedah said, smiling broadly, hopefully.

Mary positioned herself so she could again watch the deaf boy. The hookers had sandwiched him at their table. They were going at his ears. Mary could see the glistening wetness of their mouths with each kiss and nibble. The boy looked confused, his eyes darting like bugs in jars. Mary knew what the hookers would smell like to the boy: the heavy funk of artificial cherry, like in air freshener or pie filling. Or maybe rotting perfume, necrotic flowers. Their dutiful tongues would be surprisingly cold in his ears, and up close the boy could probably see their thick makeup, base the color of Silly Putty. Gunked-up eyelashes, breath tasting and smelling of fast food. Mary decided that someone had bought the hookers for the boy, and this person was forcing him to go through with it.

THE LAST SHOT of tequila slid down smoothly, missed her tongue. No need for limes. She gulped the accompanying beer anyway, so they could get going. The boy and the hookers had left.

"I want out of here," Mary said. "Let's get food somewhere."

"We could walk across the street and check out the carnival," Freedah said. "Might be fun."

"I hate carnivals," Mary said. "Especially that one." The carnival was in the sprawling parking lot of Puchi's department store more often than not. Dangerous rides churning in the sky; too many candy-colored lights; heavy, greasy wafts of corn dogs and fried bread. What were they celebrating all the time? Like her neighbors two houses down with the perpetual garage sale—every Saturday morning, the same busted vacuum cleaner, chipped dinnerware, travel magazines, golf shoes, and tired orange sofa with a stained cushion.

When she stood, Mary realized she'd need Freedah's support to walk around. "Help?" she said as she leaned heavily on Freedah's shoulder. The bar slanted and fixed itself over and over.

In the dirt parking lot, one of the hookers rested against a wide-hipped pickup with her head tilted back, lavishly working a cigarette, spraying her smoke into the purple night sky. Mary heard the feral panting and grunting of the deaf boy and realized he and the other hooker were in the cab of the truck.

"Told you he was happy," Freedah said.

"Sad," Mary said, thinking the boy should be at the

Arizona School for the Deaf and Blind, down there on
Speedway and Grande: historic, bone-white mission-style
architecture, and plush, manicured lawns of ryegrass so
green, it glowed like something atomic. She had been there
once when Chigger's team played them in baseball. After the
game, she strolled around the campus, checked out the students' paintings tacked up outside the art room, watched
two blind girls walk from the auditorium to the Coke
machine without a stumble. The deaf boy in the truck
should have a cute deaf girlfriend, a deaf cheerleader of his
own, signing away at basketball games, performing back
handsprings in saddle shoes.

"He's getting some," Freedah said. "He's happy."

"Sad."

A LINE OF homegirls in blue satin jackets stood in front of
Mary and Freedah. BARRIO ANITA was stitched across their
backs in menacing crimson thread. The girls' bangs were
sprayed and teased into stiff fans, and they cracked their
gum violently. Dazzling blinks and spins of light filled the
sky. And then there was Freedah. Her voice rose above the
jumbled din of screams, tumbling bottles, and humming
rides: "I can't believe it's only fifty cents a ticket." Mary concentrated on the strobing TILT-A-WHIRL sign above the
homegirls and again reminded herself to stop at the supermarket on the way home. In addition to the groceries, she'd
buy new bandages and antibiotic ointment for Chigger's
wound.

The scene of the hammer attack she had imagined earlier
while sitting in the bar, she realized, was flawed. Chigger's
friend Freddy had been there in the morning, peeking
up from his bowl of Raisin Bran, watching the argument,

sniggering, hearing everything, probably planning on reporting back to his own mother. He must've slept over and seen the skirmish the night before. She was lucky she wasn't in jail, lucky to be out in the cool March night, drunk, at this carnival. She pictured the article on the bottom-right corner of the front page of the *Arizona Daily Star:* TUCSON MOTHER ATTACKS TEENAGE SON WITH HAMMER.

This ride would make Mary sick—it spun, scrambled. But before she could prevent it, Freedah tugged her into a red seat shaped like a half-egg. The seat had wheels, tracked on a wavy wooden deck, and was attached with spidering cables and metal arms to a hissing set of greasy cogs and pistons in the center. "This'll be a hoot," Freedah said. The padded bar rested lightly on their laps with a clicking sound. Mary felt trapped.

Painted in slick, wet primary colors on the headrest, next to where Freedah leaned her spiral perm, was a deranged clown. It looked as if the clown was whispering something to Freedah, his exaggerated cartoon lips pushing out a foul secret.

Mary didn't want this. She wanted a hot dog with brilliant yellow mustard—anything salty. She tickled with energy and lifted the bar off her legs. Freedah tried to pull her back down, but Mary calmly said "No" and shoved Freedah's head against the clown. "You're not making me." As Mary wrestled out of her seat, the engine squealed into gear and she toppled.

Mary heard one of the homegirls yell, "That bitch is fucked! Stooopit!"

HER RIGHT LEG looked like a big Q-Tip. The part halfway up her shin—where it had been severed by the carnival ride—was wrapped in a bulb of bandage the size and shape of a watermelon. No more foot, no more ankle. Mary was relieved it was covered in a ball of bandage. The thought of seeing the stump sent waves of nausea through her stomach, made her throat clench and her eyes burn.

An IV ran from a suspended bag of piss-yellow liquid to her arm. Another tube entered the same arm: morphine that Mary could administer herself with the patient-controlled-analgesia pump. "Whenever you feel pain, press that button, and the PCA will give you just the right amount," Dr. Singh had told Mary that morning as she awakened from confusing half-dreams of arguing with Chigger. Dr. Singh was a youngish Indian man with a perfect part combed into the side of his head. He spoke quickly, spit some. "And it won't let you overdo it, so don't worry." He detailed how they had administered the initial anesthesia with a tube placed directly into her windpipe: "You were so drunk, we thought you might vomit up your stomach contents into the mask." They had also given her two blood transfusions and subjected her to numerous X rays.

Her damaged leg was numb and blubbery feeling, like she had slept on it or sat funny on a long bus trip. It was held up by a miniature hammock that hung from the jungle gym above her bed. Instead of resting, she lay queasy with a pasty mouth, under fluorescent lights in the windowless hospital room, staring at her left toes, wiggling them.

A nurse walked in. Her shoes squeaked like baby toys on the shiny floor. Mary glanced down at the nurse's legs. She wore green scrubs and all-white jogging shoes.

"Oh, you're awake again," the nurse said. "We called your son's school, and he reported to homeroom right on time this morning, so you don't have to worry about him."

Chigger was never tardy; she hadn't been worrying about

that. "Where's my leg?" Mary asked. For the better part of the morning, after she received phone calls from her distressed cousin and brother who lived in Douglas near the Mexican border, she had been vividly recalling a ceremony she had attended as a child down in Bisbee.

Her grandfather, who had been a copper miner, had his hand torn off when he caught it in the gears of a conveyor belt. On a rare drizzly day in April, with the healthy smell of creosote saturating the wind, they buried the hand in the family's plot on a low hill in the cemetery that overlooked La Iglesia San Judas Tadeo. A stone marker, a miniature gravestone, was sunk into the wet earth: RIGHT HAND OF GEORGE IAN GRIFFIN, LOST 12 APRIL 1959. The same priest who had heard Mary's first confession, Padre Diaz, mumbled a few Latin prayers and made the sign of the cross on her grandfather's forehead before her uncle William shoveled mud over the little wooden box he had fashioned for his father's hand.

A wave of compassion washed across the nurse's ruddy face before she composed herself. "Didn't Dr. Singh go over that with you this morning?" The nurse reached for Mary's hand. "You've lost some . . . just below—"

"I know that," Mary said, pulling her hand away. "What did they do with the part they cut off? Where is it?"

"What? Why?"

"It needs to be saved. Where is it?"

"The surgeons tried, but they couldn't—"

"Where is it?"

The nurse squinted at Mary and left the room. A few moments later, Dr. Singh bustled in with an X ray and reintroduced himself. Then he started: "Your foot and ankle were tangled up in the wheels and gears and such." He spread the X ray on a lighted wall panel and pointed at the blue and gray image with a pen. "The wheel cut clean through right here. This is the fibula, and this is the tibia. . . ."

Mary waited for him to stop jabbering, then said, "Where are they?"

"What?" Dr. Singh said.

"My ankle and foot."

"Why?"

"They're mine," Mary said. She remembered trudging back to the pickup trucks after her grandfather's hand funeral, her patent-leather shoes sucking the mud, her white tights soaking up the brown water from puddles. She asked her aunt Siobhan what would have happened if her grandfather's hand had been lost down in the mine, if they had never found it. "How'd you like to go to Heaven with only one hand?" her aunt snapped. She tugged Mary along by Mary's hood, and scolded her for muddying herself.

"It needs to be properly buried," Mary told Dr. Singh. She squirmed and adjusted the pillows under her shoulders. "I remembered this morning after you left."

"They were properly disposed of," Dr. Singh said, "like all biohazardous materials."

"That's not what I meant," Mary said, and she reached for the television remote control on the small table next to her bed. She aimed it at the ceiling-mounted TV and pressed the on/off button several times before Dr. Singh spoke again: "You have to pay for TV here."

AN HOUR LATER, there was a faint knocking on her opened door. She clicked off the buzzing TV.

"I'm Father MacKay," the man in the door said. "You have some questions regarding your foot."

"I just want a proper burial for it," Mary said, looking over at him optimistically. "That's all, Father."

Father MacKay pulled a plastic chair up to Mary's bed. "It must be very difficult for you."

"Just want a proper burial."

The priest's eyes were lake blue, his face, fleshy and white. He never goes outside, Mary thought. He never leaves this bright hospital world.

"There's no such ceremony in the Roman ritual," he said. "I promise."

"There was a funeral for my grandfather's hand," Mary said. "Even a special gravestone."

He took her hand in his and looked into her eyes with the deliberation of a patient kindergarten teacher. "A foot is not an essential part of a person. It wouldn't be appropriate to have a funeral for the person or any nonessential part of the person if the person hasn't died." His palm was moist and much softer than hers.

"There was one for my grandfather's hand."

"Where was this?" He thumbed his chin.

"Two hours south of here in Bisbee."

"One might innovate a ceremony for psychological mollification," Father MacKay said, "but no formal rite exists for the burial of lost limbs."

Mary noticed Chigger at the door. He clutched a single white rose and rolled his eyes. The Band-Aid on his neck was brown—it needed to be changed. He wore a green Mulligan Pirates baseball cap. The catcher. His coach had told Mary that he could throw from home plate to second faster than most college players. "Arm like a rocket," the coach had boasted.

"Take off your hat, Chigger," Mary said. "This is Father MacKay."

Mary watched Father MacKay as he turned to greet Chigger. He sported the same bemused and disgusted expression everyone sported when they first met Chigger: eyebrows perked, mouth slightly ajar—like they had just swallowed a bug. Who is this hulking, furry man in boy's clothes? Besides the cap, Chigger wore baggy shorts and a tight black T-shirt with a cracking white print of a fish skeleton silk-screened across the chest.

"Father, this is my son Chigger," Mary said, quickly enough to avoid Father MacKay's asking something awkward, like was Chigger her husband or boyfriend.

Father MacKay stood, shook Chigger's hand, and turned back to Mary. "I can come back later and anoint you." Before Mary could say anything else, the priest left, squeezing by Chigger.

Chigger handed her the white rose and sat in the plastic chair. Mary knew he had most likely stolen the flower, but she loved it. She smelled it and placed it on the cluttered table next to her bed. "Why aren't you at school? Who took you here?"

"I took Roger's truck," Chigger said. "It's a stick-shifter, but I only stalled once. Your car's dead, of course." Chigger scratched near the wound on his neck, then looked at his finger. "Freedah stayed over last night. She came with a policeman at two in the morning and woke me up."

Mary knew she should say something to Chigger about driving. She figured he'd be nailed by the cops one of these times, but right now she didn't care; she appreciated that he was here, not even complaining about the hole she might have torn in his neck.

"And I'm not allowed to go back to school until Tuesday," he added.

"Why?"

"These guys, Jason and Todd, they were trying to make Grace eat dog shit they scooped with a plastic bag, so I kicked their asses."

"Didn't you tell the principal that?" Mary said. "Making someone eat dog shit is much worse." Her leg was beginning to tingle, but it didn't bother her as much as the image of the two mean boys trying to force Grace, one of Chigger's two friends, to eat dog shit. She did wish Chigger would find other friends, normal kids to hang around. This Grace wore cottony maternity dresses that she'd cut off with scissors way above the knees, and boots: big, clunky army boots. Chigger's other friend, Freddy, the boy who might have witnessed the hammer attack, wore normal clothes, but there was something shifty about him—his frenetic machine-gun laugh, the spastic twitching of his chin, the fact that Mary had once discovered him in her bathroom sniffing her slipper.

"I told Mr. Cannel, but I beat up the same kids last week, too, so he was extra mad." Chigger looked up over his shoulder at the dormant TV. "Sorry about your leg," he said. "I bet you were drunk, though, so you didn't really feel it, right?" He turned back to his mother.

"I was in shock, Chiggy. I don't remember," Mary said. She pressed the red morphine button with her thumb and anticipated the magic washing through her.

"Was it that dumb redneck who made you go on the ride?" Chigger asked.

"Clem wasn't even there," Mary said. "I was with Freedah."

"You'll get a fake foot, right? And you can walk, right?"

"They have special doctors for that," Mary said. "I'll work with one to find the right thing."

"You told the priest you want to bury your foot," Chigger said. "Will they let you?"

"No," Mary said. "But Father MacKay says it's not important." But she saw herself in Heaven, stumbling through clouds on crutches. Or maybe a saint would deliver her foot on a velvet pillow as she crossed over. "What're you doing with the rest of your week?"

As he stood and put his cap back over his Bozo-red hair, Chigger said, "I'll be here." Mary noticed his eyes were glazed in wetness and his nose was running. "But now I have to pick up Grace at her piano lesson and get Roger's truck back."

"Before you go, we could have the nurse look at your neck and change the Band-Aid."

"It's fine," Chigger said, sniffing. "And you really didn't do it to me. The Petronis' dog chased me into their barbed-wire fence." Chigger lumbered out of the room but poked his head back in. "I'll be here again tomorrow morning."

"Careful driving," Mary yelled after him. She wished she could believe the barbed-wire story. She'd try.

ON HER THIRD DAY in the hospital, Mary was visited by an occupational therapist who carried a gym bag full of prosthetic choices; a psychologist who suggested that Mary breathe deeply and repeat "I am a whole person"; an insurance specialist from the VA who tirelessly helped her pore over an hour's worth of forms; various doctors and nurses; and Freedah, who had brought Mary a stack of water-damaged romance magazines and a get-well Mylar balloon bearing the image of a cartoon dinosaur hugging a heart.

"I think you're obsessing about this foot funeral business because you don't want to face the fact that you're handicapped now," Freedah said. "Remember how I obsessed about my makeup when I first got my perm?"

Mary pressed the PCA button. The night before, she had

considered the morphine coursing through her veins, making her sleepy, soft. The drug seemed dangerous and illegal—fun. She closed her eyes and waited for the tiny stars.

"I heard something affirming," Freedah said. "They're calling it handi*capable,* not handi*capped.* Isn't that great?"

"Great," Mary said. She pushed the button again and faded a little until she smelled wet hay and feed pellets. She opened her eyes and looked over Freedah's mop of curls to see Roger. He stood under the TV and held a wrapped package the size of boxed candy. At work, at the feed store, she didn't notice Roger's smell; he smelled right among the chickens and sacks of fertilizer. She noticed his smell now—musty and musky. She sort of liked it. He handed her the gift. She could see his grubby fingerprints on the Scotch tape. "Thanks, Roger."

"It's nothing," Roger said. He took off his sweaty cap. His thick, rusty hair was stuck to his head. Mary wanted to shampoo it, comb out the snarls with cream rinse.

"Let me," Freedah said. She snatched the present from Mary and quickly ripped off the paper. "A cookbook. *Southwestern Barbecuing,*" she announced. "Hmmph."

"Thanks, Roger," Mary said. She began to feel the morphine oozing through her like warm sauce.

"With the price sticker still on. Reduced to $1.99," Freedah said. "Classy, Roger."

"I didn't know what to get," he said. He pulled up a chair. "I got you twenty pounds of ribs, too. Chigger packed them good into your freezer."

"Thanks," Mary said. "I'll have a party when I get out of here."

She looked at Roger's shirt, a white snap-pocketed Western job with brown tobacco stains down the front. She knew she could get the stains out with lemon juice and the sun, and she would the next time he stayed over. Roger was one of the few men she had fooled around with since Chigger's father died eight years before.

Not counting Roger, Mary's latest beau had been Clem, the reason Chigger had called her a man-at-the-dog-track-screwing whore. When Clem first moseyed up to Mary and Freedah a few weeks ago at the Finish Line Bar and Grill—his bright green-gray eyes, his cleft chin like a perfect little butt—Mary had assumed he'd be asking Freedah to two-step. He asked Mary instead, and she spent the next hour with her hand pried into the back pocket of his Wranglers, inhaling his deliciously antiseptic cologne.

Chigger had seen Mary and Clem emerge from her bedroom a few mornings as he sat at the table eating his cereal. Chigger never said anything to Clem except for the last such morning, when he grumbled "dumb hickoid" in Clem's direction.

And that night, as Mary and Clem were feeding their left-over scraps of dinner to the stinky javelinas snorting around the wooden stoop of Clem's duplex, Clem complained, "That Sasquatch in your kitchen is beginning to chap my hide." He tossed a strip of fat to a youngish pig. The animal looked like a keg.

Chigger had done the same thing to Roger at first, but Roger had never said anything mean. Instead, he brought gifts for Chigger, made him breakfast, went to his ball games.

"What'd you call my Chigger?" Mary said to Clem.

"Sasquatch," Clem said. "That kid's a fucking Big Foot."

Mary pinched a wad of gristle off her plate and flung it at Clem. It hit his temple with a wet slap and stuck: a gray, greasy leech. She stepped off the heel-gnawed porch into the dirt, kicked through the grubbing swine, and walked three miles to a gas station, where she called Roger for a ride.

She and Roger were more buddies than lovers. They drank and gambled on the Indian reservations together. They went to the titty bars. Thursdays, Roger usually met Mary and Freedah at the dog track. Sometimes he'd drive Mary home, and they'd park in the dust behind the feed store. Their sex wasn't hot and passionate; it was somewhat perfunctory, but friendly and fun. In the truck with the crackly radio tuned to country classics, Mary'd pleasure Roger with the equivalent intentions she had when she fixed him supper after work, and Roger would bring Mary to orgasm with the same loyalty he demonstrated when he helped her clean the carburetor of her jalopy.

Whenever Roger stayed over at Mary's, she'd draw him a bath, squirting liquid soap under the running water, and scrub off the day's work with a boar brush. She'd clip his nails, shave the hair that grew down the back of his browned neck with her pink razor, and sprinkle baby powder over his milky white shoulders, working them like dough. They'd sleep together on crisp, line-dried sheets that smelled cool and open.

But the sex there was never as fun as the truck sex. Both of them were more at ease in the truck; they'd move with less thought in the truck. Mary would weave one bare leg through the steering wheel, not caring if she honked the horn, and Roger would dive into her until her toes fisted up, and she'd say, "I owe you one."

Neither cared—or let on that they cared—if the other was screwing around.

Mary wondered now if Roger would steer his truck behind the feed store after the races on Thursday nights. She doubted it. He'd be afraid he might catch a glimpse of the stump.

MARY WAS DISCHARGED from the hospital on day eleven. The dressing on her leg wasn't as big as before, but it was still ugly and cumbersome—it looked like a blue boxing glove without the thumb. Chigger had called it a Smurf boot when he first saw it.

Neither Freedah nor Roger could fetch Mary until late, so Mary decided to let Chigger take Roger's truck after school and come rescue her from the boredom of the hospital. As she waited for Chigger, she practiced figure eights in her temporary wheelchair, pumping the wheels with her arms and shoulders, gliding on the slick white floor in a quiet section of the hall she had discovered near the service elevators. Just when she thought she was getting the hang of it, pirouetting in smaller and smaller circles, she crashed into a metal cart laden with cleansers and bedpans. A small vial of liquid shattered on the floor with a pop. Mary rolled away from the mess.

Chigger and Grace stood outside Mary's room. Chigger carried Mary's things: an overnight bag, a few magazines. "You all set?" he said.

"Sure," Mary said. "Roger's truck okay?"

"Yup," Chigger said. "And I didn't stall once."

"You almost stalled in the parking lot," Grace said to Chigger. Then she turned to Mary and said, "Hi."

Mary noticed the word *emancipation* scrawled in black marker across the front of Grace's flimsy, frayed dress, just above the waist. "What's that all about?" Mary asked, pointing to the word.

"It means I busted free from stuff," Grace said. Grace looked down at her dress and pulled the fabric taut so the word was bigger. She smiled at the word.

"She did it in art," Chigger said.

"Chigger did something in art," Grace said.

"Shut up," Chigger told Grace. He shoved her, and she shoved him back—pretty forceful for a skinny girl. The magazines spilled from his grasp and flopped onto the floor. Chigger and Grace laughed.

IN THE BLAZING parking lot, as Chigger pushed Mary's wheelchair and Grace skipped ahead, showing the world her frilly panties, a sickening series of thoughts raced through Mary's mind. This would be the first time she rode in Roger's truck with one foot. The first time she entered her house with one foot. The first time she opened her refrigerator with one foot. The first time she cracked a beer with one foot. She remembered Freedah's comment about handi*capable,* looked down at her Smurf boot, and choked out a cry.

Grace twirled around and squatted in front of the wheelchair. "Don't," she said. "We're taking you somewhere."

"I'm not," Mary said between rough sobs, blotting her tears with the straps of the canvas bag Chigger had plopped on her lap. "Take me home."

MARY SAT BY the window. Grace straddled the stick shift with her gangly legs. The wheelchair was folded in the bed of the truck among Roger's rusted gardening implements.

Chigger changed gears at the correct times, even downshifted, and braked like he had been driving the truck for years—no jolts, no swerves, and no stalls as they cruised by piñata stores and taco shacks. And the whole time, he calmly bobbed his head to the radio.

Mary turned down the music and said, "You're driving real good, Chig, but can we please just go home?"

"Nope," Chigger said. "We can't."

When they turned westward on Miracle Mile, Mary knew Chigger was taking her to Evergreen Cemetery. Chuck, Chigger's father, had died in a car wreck when Chigger was five, but Mary had only been to his gravesite a few times. Chuck had been an air force pilot, flying million-dollar jets, parachuting three times per month. Chuck knew how to shoot big guns and scuba dive. For fun he and his buddies used to get blind drunk and smash through class-four rapids on the Salt River, clinging to old army surplus rafts and whooping it up. Then, one hot July afternoon, as Chuck pulled out of the parking lot of the doughnut shop two blocks from their house, a UPS truck flattened his Ford Fairmont sedan.

Evergreen Cemetery—where Chuck had ended up—was homely. The towering umbrella palms looked out of place, like dinosaur movie props, and the grass was always crispy and brown. Mary decided that if she ever got rich, she'd have Chuck's body exhumed and reburied in the little graveyard in Bisbee.

"Chigger," Mary said, "I really don't want to go to your father's grave right now."

"We have to," Chigger said.

"We have to," Grace repeated.

"Chigger!" Mary screamed. Her ears popped, and she heard a sandy noise in her head. "You're not making me go there."

Chigger pulled the truck into the parking lot of a convenience store, a yellow cinder-block building. The truck shuddered and stalled, and Chigger hit the steering wheel with his meaty fist. It honked. "I made a box for you," Chigger said. "In art."

Mary looked blankly at the giant vivid posters of burritos and hamburgers on the wall in front of the truck. "Please take me home now," she said. "My leg hurts, and I'm supposed to keep it raised." She lied about it hurting.

Grace reached over Mary's lap and clicked open the glove compartment. She pulled out a decorated shoebox. The lid was painted in thick blues and whites to look like a cloudy sky, the sides were black and starry. She lifted the lid off the box and revealed a soiled sneaker. "Chigger got your shoe from the nurse," Grace said. No one had cleaned off the dried blood, and a gamy odor was set loose in the truck.

"It's the left shoe," Chigger said. "They tossed the right one with your foot. This one was in a biohazard plastic bag, but the nurse gave it to me, anyway."

"Chigger and I even tried to sneak into the part of the hospital where they throw away legs," Grace said. "We got to one room where a guy in a white space suit yelled at us."

"They burn them," Mary said. "Like trash."

"We were going to bury the shoe next to Chuck," Chigger said. "I made the coffin."

"I love the coffin," Mary said, taking it from Grace, feeling the different layers of paint, each star a nub. "I love it." She put the lid back on, covering the ugliness and stink of the bloody shoe with the partly cloudy skyscape.

"Now what're we gonna do with it?" Chigger said.

"The shoe's a symbol," Grace said.

"Duh," Chigger said. "I think she knows that."

"I love this coffin," Mary said. She tried to think of a place as beautiful as the box where they could bury it.

. . .

MARY LAY IN the sweet, rich grass behind the dugout, barely escaping the spotty shadow of her wheelchair. She felt the moistness of the overwatered lawn seeping through her T-shirt and shorts, but she didn't care. She sucked in the coolness, combed the grass with her bare left toes, and sniffed. She rolled on her side, looked over at the white archways, the students spilling through them. There were plenty of cute deaf girls for the deaf boy, all in bright, neat clothes, all talking as quickly with their hands as most kids their age talked with their mouths. None of the students looked across the grass at her or Grace or Chigger. And Chigger was digging behind their home plate, the crunch of the shovel audible above the clamor of the final-bell bustle. Mary rolled flat on her back again, closed her eyes, and saw the orange sun pushing through her eyelids.

She opened her eyes when the orange stopped. Chigger stood above her, blocking the sun, his legs thick as logs, his head small in the sky. "Come watch us bury it," he said. His sideburns curled outward like flames. "Roger said to have you home by five. He's barbecuing ribs for us before he takes you to the track."

Chigger scratched around his neck wound. From down there, Mary could see under the loosening Band-Aid: dark, scabbed over. It'll scar, she thought. It'll scar bad. She'd wheel over to the Petronis' yard tomorrow and check for that barbed wire.

"Roger's taking me to the track?" Mary asked, extending her hand so Chigger could help her up. "Really?"

a note on the author

Mark Poirier was born and grew up in Arizona, the fifth of eleven children. He studied at the Iowa Writers' Workshop and received a Michener Fellowship. He is the author of the novel GOATS, also published by Bloomsbury.

acknowledgments

I'd like to thank Bill U'Ren, Stephen Dixon, John Barth, and Judith Grossman for help with these stories.

For encouragement and support, thanks to Larry McMurtry, Diana Ossana, Fred Haefele, Andrew Wylie, Sarah Chalfant, Jin Auh, Hilary Bass, Deb West, Ben Niehart, Madison Smartt Bell, Carolyn Grossman, Karla Kuban, Malinda McCollum, Jeff and Brandy Poirier, and my parents.

c r e d i t s

"Monkey Chow" first appeared in *Aethlon: The Journal of Sport Literature,* Summer 1995.

"Bear, Bikes, Bug-Boy" first appeared in *Green Mountains Review,* Fall/ Winter 1995–1996.

"Before the Barbecue Hoedown" first appeared in *Gulf Coast,* Summer/ Fall 1996.

"Pray for Beans" first appeared in *Coe Review: Annual Experimental Literary Anthology,* May 1997.

"La Zona Roja" first appeared in *BOMB,* June 1997.

"Cul-de-sacs" first appeared in *Manoa: A Pacific Journal of International Writing,* Fall 1997.

"Tilt-a-Whirl" first appeared in *Laurel Review,* Fall 1997.

"Disciplinary Log" first appeared as "Mulligan Junior High School Disciplinary Log" in *JANE,* November 1998.